Burnt Corn & Other Creepy Stories

GARY R. LOWELL

Full Moon Publishing, LLC

Glade Spring, VA

Website http://www.fullmoonpublishingllc.com

Cover Designer Danielle Stamper

ISBN: 1946232068
ISBN-13: 978-1946232069

CONTENTS

ACKNOWLEDGMENTS

The author sincerely expresses his gratitude to Patricia Wood Dickerson for extracting time from her busy scientific writing schedule to read early versions of all of the stories in this volume, offering valuable suggestions for their improvement, soothing the writer's insecurities and writing a too-generous preface for the collection.

Preface to Burnt Corn & Other Creepy Stories

This handful of polished nuggets is panned from a life stream that has meandered from the Alaskan outback to steamy, seamy Belem, and from world capitols to California cotton patches. Lowell's images are perceptive and authentic, and his characters -- whether enraged baboons, lovelorn songbirds, debauched urbanites or spikey plants -- engage you immediately in their tales. *Burnt Corn & Other Creepy Stories* is an adventure in juxtaposition: venues from Yokosuka, Japan to Tequila, Mexico; characters from amorous jackrabbits to wily dealers in jewels; architecture from the grand aqueduct of Coimbra to rabbit hutches in rural Alabama. Each nugget shines on its own, and the collection is a treasure trove.

Patricia Wood Dickerson

BURNT CORN

I would have to guess that you have never heard of Burnt Corn, Alabama, but no matter, neither had I until my arrival there by parcel post express. History tells us that Burnt Corn was settled by white folks as a trading post within the Creek Indian Nation shortly after the Revolutionary War at the historic intersection of Three Notch Trail and Old Wolf Path. This relic of colonial times is situated in southern Alabama, about 10-miles northeast of modern Monroeville, at the mutual intersection of state highways 30, 15, and 5. It lies between the Alabama River on the east and the Conecuh River on the west. My story takes place in recent times at the Acme Rabbitry which is, of course, to be found in Burnt Corn.

My reception in Burnt Corn was unceremonious to say the least. My shipping carton was plunked down on a counter in the small post office next to another box filled with 100 peeping baby chicks at about 3 a.m. Evidently, a phone call was made, and some hour and a half later, my crate was tossed into the back of a pickup truck which traversed roads of declining quality until we arrived at what I later learned was the Acme Rabbitry.

My initial impression of Burnt Corn and the Acme Rabbitry was dominated by the awful smell of hundreds of rabbits, the odor of their excrement and urine wafting through an aqueous atmosphere one could almost drink. I did not like the place or its name. However, I was placed, by my ears, into a distant quarantine cage which, at least, provided a bowl of water which I desperately needed. It had been a long and thirsty 1,200-miles from Socorro, New Mexico to Burnt Corn, Alabama.

Since you probably know nothing about our kind beyond the Easter myth, permit me to edify you on the difference between hares and rabbits. Oh yes, I quite appreciate the similarities between the two, both have wonderfully soft fur, long twitching whiskers, wiggly noses, cute puffy tails, prominent incisors and long ears. But I assure you, long ears alone do not make a rabbit, and I should know, because I am a *Lepus californicus*, a western, black-tailed jack rabbit, which is a calumnious misnaming. I am a hare, long, lean and fast as a bullet which rabbits are definitely not. At top speed I am capable of graceful leaps of 20 feet or more and right-angle turns in the blink of an eye.

The order Lagomorpha includes the family Leporidae which encompasses both hares and rabbits but there the similarity ends, taxonomically speaking. The common squatty, plump domestic rabbits descend from the wild European rabbit, *Oryctlagus cuniculus*, named by Linnaeus in 1758. They made their first appearance during the Middle Ages as table fare and now there are 28 species of these chubby critters in the genus *Oryctlagus*. Hares, on the other hand, comprise 30 species in the genus *Lepus*. But enough of this science, let me tell you my story.

Although you might not suspect it, since Leporids are naturally so taciturn, but these creatures are capable of making a multiplicity of sounds in the form of squeals, grunts and snuffles that actually comprise a simple language. I know it surprises humans to hear that these timid, long-eared, innocent beings are capable of articulate speech and modestly intellectual thought. In the case of rabbits, however, their philosophy leans toward the far-left ideals of social democrats; they love their safe, confining hutches and meals that come without cost or labor on their part, but they fail to recognize that these benefits come at the price of being southern fried at a young age.

Hares, in contrast, are the ultimate loners, wandering across large tracts of the farm lands and high deserts of the southwest in pursuit of food and avoidance of predators. Most hares incline towards right-wing thinking with the exception of their stance on gun-politics. Without exception, hares abhor guns of any kind, even toy guns. So, as you can see, hares and rabbits share very little in common, outside of long ears, and as a rule they are not overly fond of each other and seldom have social intercourse.

No doubt you have noticed that the eyes of both rabbits and hares are side-mounted and set 180 degrees apart to provide a 360-degree field of vision. In the case of jack rabbits, like myself, we have black pupils set in yellow-ochre irises and our eyes are especially adept at detecting motion at a distance. Humans often remark on our graceful leaping ability which allows us to clear sage brush, calculate our escape route and note the progress of any pursuers.

We have also an excellent sense of smell and the length of our ears tells all when it comes to hearing. Did you know that most rabbits, and all hares, sleep with eyes open and ears laid back? You might also have noticed that they often twitch during dreams and stop wiggling their noses. Of course, the slightest noise or movement brings them to instant alertness. All of these evolutionary attributes are defensive, of course, none of us would last an hour in the wild without them in the face of fierce coyotes, dogs, bobcats, horned owls, hawks, foxes, snakes and even feral cats.

Juvenile rabbits are called "kittens" or "kits", not bunnies, please! Baby hares are termed "leverets" and are born, after a gestation of 43 days, opened-eyed, furred and capable of evasive movement and squeals if danger threatens. Mother hares hide their young from predators in sites that change frequently. In contrast, domestic kits are born in fur-lined nests, naked, closed-eyed and totally helpless after a gestation of only 31 days. For domestic rabbits, fur appears in about two days, the eyes open in about 10 days and they are usually in a skillet by 14-16 weeks. Who, then, would not prefer the open, nomadic life of a hare?

My arrival at the Acme Rabbitry disrupted the nocturnal

routine of the resident rabbits and, though I could see nothing in the darkness from my position, I easily discerned their mutterings "What has arrived?" "My God, is it a wild hare?" "What on earth is that filthy creature doing here?" "Has the master lost his mind?" and a host of similar hostile remarks which told me I was not a welcome addition to their society. Chief among these detractors was Uncle Dickie, the herd buck, whom I could distinguish by his odious smell, pronounced southern-rabbit accent and a distinct sibilance produced by overlong incisors.

The following morning, I met my new master, a professional rabbit-raiser who knew his business, but not what I would call an overly educated white man. He filled my water bowl, placed a mineral block and a wooden sitting-plank in my cage and filled my feed hopper with high quality alfalfa hay. He examined me closely through the wire netting of the cage then opened the door and took me up by the nape of the neck rather than the ears. I resisted the urge to fight back with scratching and biting; there is nothing to be gained by resisting a man who knows how to handle rabbits and who can end your life with a simple twist of your neck. He felt my body in its entirety, checked out my sex and, apparently satisfied with my form and fur, put me back in my cage.

During this examination, I could see Uncle Dickie perched on his hind legs, some 20 yards distant, following every move the master made. Dickie was of a breed called New Zealand Whites, as were all the animals falling in my circle of sight. This is a breed of albino freaks with pure white fur and red, zombie-like eyes and are entirely too fat and ugly to describe for a simple hare. After the master's departure, the obstreperous Uncle Dickie made a farting sound with his lips and clacked his incisors, evidently intending these rude antics as insults to the newcomer. It was clear that the herd buck was a redneck and a dunce and we would be enemies.

I remained in isolation for ten days but, after a second thorough examination by the master, I was placed in a hutch directly across from Uncle Dickie at the end of a long double row of hutches housing does and feeder rabbits. No sooner was the master out of sight than Dickie began regaling me with accounts of his sexual prowess and personal history, the number of does he had inseminated, the number of offspring he had generated, his knowledge of the rabbit business, his blue ribbons from the Monroe County Fair (three years running), and much, much more. The list of his accomplishments and virtues was endless, by his reckoning, and I soon perceived that this was a form of psychological warfare, a hateful, round-the-clock assault of comical, Dixie-accented, brainwashing. I turned my rear towards him, ejected thirty pellets in his honor, laid my ears back, wrinkled my forehead and glared at him with what I hoped was an evil, hateful look. These actions insulted him, as intended, and he was quiet for a few minutes before he began retelling me his life story from birth to present day. Agonizing!

Our exchange of insults, curses and pellet discharges continued for days without surcease before an exceptional event gave us both something else to think about. This was the arrival of a female rabbit, named Josephine. Josephine was a beautifully furred, silver-grey chinchilla rabbit with bright beautiful eyes and bold irises of marbled blue.

Josephine was a naïve, but educated, English-speaking, urban rabbit raised in a New York City apartment and transported to Auburn University by her mistress only to find that pet rabbits were not permitted in shared dorm rooms. Her advertisement in the local newspaper brought our rabbit master to her door and Josephine to Burnt Corn. The master wanted her very badly because of her perfect conformance to the Chinchilla standard of perfection.

Miss Josie, the southern transfiguration of her given name, courtesy of Uncle Dickie, learned to speak English from her human caregiver but had never seen another rabbit, only herself in a mirror. Consequently, she did not speak a word of the common Leporid language. She was raised as a lap rabbit with a private litter box and had certainly never beheld a nasty herd buck such as our Dickie. Miss Josie was frightened by living outdoors in a prison cage, under what she thought of as unsanitary conditions, and in proximity to coyotes and dogs who visited the rabbitry nightly.

Miss Josie endured her ten days of quarantine, required of all new arrivals, and during this interval, was subjected to lewd nocturnal soliloquies by the loquacious and rascally Uncle Dickie. This sufficed to inform all of the inhabitants of the rabbitry that she did not speak or understand our language. When her quarantine was completed, she was placed in a conventional hutch next to mine and opposite that of the malodorous herd buck. She was horrified by Dickie's pink eyes and obvious intentions and would have been further horrified if she could have understood the vile nature of his remarks.

I began teaching her our language and she learned quite quickly for, after all, it is a simple language by comparison with English or Romance languages. This one-on-one exchange also permitted me to increase my English vocabulary which consisted almost exclusively of mathematical terms like hypotenuse, double integrals, hyperbolic functions, quadratic equations, law of cosines and the like. I neglected to mention that my name is Euclid and I was raised beneath the building housing the Math Department of New Mexico Tech where I was exposed to a wide range of mathematical concepts. I would not be surprised if my understanding of the subjects expounded by the professors exceeded that of many of the dozing, glassy-eyed human students sitting above me.

At any rate, Miss Josie and I were soon able to communicate through a mixture of English and Leporid that began with an exchange of our life stories whispered through the wire separating us to exclude the rude herd buck from our conversations. Josephine complained of the primitive living conditions we endured, the heat, humidity, coarse food, the hardware cloth floors of our hutches, the lack of a private litter box and, of course, the repulsive rabbit directly opposite us.

Predictably, Uncle Dickie continually interjected his uncouth observations, the most offensive of which, was to point out that Josephine would be a herd doe, destined to be pregnant the rest of her life, and that he would necessarily be her impregnator in the very near future. Miss Josie angrily responded by telling the odious buck that she would commit suicide rather than permit any intimacy between herself and an oafish albino like him. At the time, this was the most complex sentence I had heard her utter in the Leporid language and I was extremely proud of my teaching and gratified by the effect that it produced on our obnoxious neighbor, who clacked his incisors, turned his back to us, and discharged an impressive stream of 50 pellets.

Following this unsavory exhibition, I explained to Miss Josie, as gently as I could, the maxim of "no free lunch", the realities of a commercial rabbit enterprise and that, at some point in the near future, she would be placed in the confines of repugnant Uncle Dickie's domain to become inseminated. My message was not well received and sent the lady into a tearful rage at the coarse realities of her new life. After a couple of hours of pouting, she opened a conversation which led to a frank discussion of rabbit vegetarianism versus the uncivilized, carnivorous habits of humans, wealth and poverty, and the contrasts between socialism and capitalism. This colloquy ended in more tears and with nasty chortling on the part of the turpitudinous buck. Josephine was an unhappy rabbit.

The next morning, Miss Josie began whispering excitedly to me that she had conceived a solution to her problems and that I was to be the key player in her new plan. She told me that she accepted the idea of "No free lunch" and that she would have to be "mated" (she used this word in English), bear young and become a productive member of the Acme Rabbitry. I was on the point of congratulating her on accepting the realities of the situation when she went on to say that her plan revolved around *me* as the mate in question. I did not know what to say, it was obvious that she had no background in genetic science. I pointed out that we were of different species, even of different genera, and producing live, unflawed offspring was unlikely, if not impossible, and might well lead to the death of both of us. I insisted that what she was proposing went against nature's plan, was counter to evolutionary doctrine, and could only end in heartbreak, and, mayhap, death for both of us.

"Are you saying that love and happiness are impossible between hare and rabbit?" she demanded petulantly. "I overheard the master saying to one of his workers that he thinks it is possible and, not only that, I think he is obsessed with the idea implanted by a TV show about breeding male lions and female tigers to obtain the large, beautiful cats called *ligers*."

This suggested to me that Josephine and I were here in Burnt Corn, amidst a population of albinos, for inter-genus experimentation in hybridization. It sounded positively Naziesque. I pointed out to Josephine that lions and tigers were both members of the *Panthera* genus and that what she was proposing, and what the master was evidently contemplating, was a cross-genus affair and would almost certainly not produce acceptable results. I restrained myself from calculating the statistical probability of success in such an experiment but she seemed to have read my mind. "I know the odds are against us, dear Euclid, but I am willing to take the chance to avoid becoming a sex slave of that filthy, villainous rabbit sitting across from us. I would rather die than submit to him" she responded passionately.

The rakish Uncle Dickie heard the last remark and, of course, had to interject "When master delivers you to me, be prepared for the mother of all romping's, little Miss Josie from New York!"

When master did come by, on his daily check of the automated water system, he found Miss Josie posed on her hind legs, front paws folded and crossed and twiddling her whiskers in a most charming manner. She cut an insanely adorable figure. She began speaking to him in English (I neglected to mention that when rabbits and hares do speak, it is in very subdued and hushed tones) and the master was obliged to kneel on the ground and put his ear to the confining wire to catch her words. She expressed her willingness to attempt an experiment in hybrid reproduction with me and predicted our offspring would inherit my long body combined with her meatiness and quality fur which was in demand by the fur trade. She did not have to mention ligers.

Uncle Dickie overheard this conversation, of course, but as he could not understand a word of English, he assumed that Miss Josie was expressing discontent at the prospect of mating with him and, feeling this an insult, began snorting and thumping his hind foot in angry protest. I was able to follow her conversation and was shocked by the scope of the lady's bold gamble in addressing our human master. Conversation with humans is simply not in the Leporid play book. I was concerned with our mutual safety but it was plain to see that the commercial implications of such a hybrid struck immediate favor with the master. It married well with his preconceived desire to be the creator who brings a new breed of Leporid to the rabbit fancy.

I might just say, here, that the master was a graduate of the Animal Science Department of the prestigious Auburn University, but his course of study did not include training in genetics, but, perhaps, that is already obvious. That evening, he conceived, on his own, that possession of a talking Chinchilla rabbit was an equally remunerative aspect of the proposed experiment, even if it failed to produce a new breed. The master, inspired by the public success of the *Panthera leo* x *Panthera tigris* hybrid, occupied himself until late hours inventing novel names for his new breed. *Leporbit, Raborid,* and *Leporyx* would be examples of his originality.

From my perspective, the union would certainly fail to conceive anything, and certainly not hybrids with favorable traits, and the lives of the buck and doe would be forfeit. As a jack rabbit, I knew that I could fake symptoms of tularemia, the dreaded rabbit fever, which would save me from the stewpot but rush me to summary execution and cremation. This dilemma forced me to briefly consider an escape plan and life in the wild for the mismatched pair, but poor Josephine seemed to be woefully incapable of life on the ground.

During the early morning hours, an idea came to me that revolved around a wager with the rabbit master and would require my mathematical expertise. I knew the master was an "aggie" and, consequently, knew nothing about elementary mathematics. I could pose the famous "rabbit problem" to him in exchange for my freedom and an open, accessible cage for Josephine in daylight hours that would be closed each night for safety. Best of all, it would provide freedom of the open road for the me, if he could not solve the riddle. We would then promise to conduct our reproductive work, in full view of all, during the day.

I acquainted Josephine with my plan and she approved but worried that the master might be able to solve the problem. I gave her assurances that this was extremely unlikely and that my concern was that the master might not keep his word if he lost the bet. Her view was that his desire for a new hybrid would compel him to honor his word, if he lost. So it was agreed to lay our proposition before the master at the earliest opportunity.

On the next morning, the master found both Josephine and myself perched on our hind legs with dangling front paws and whiskers a-twiddling. We wanted to be at our cutest when we opened a negotiation that our lives might depend on. We broached our plan in English to exclude the depraved Dickie, who had his ears plastered to the wire of his hutch. The master was quite pleased to find that he had both a talking rabbit and a talking hare in his possession and was brimming with confidence. As a professional breeder, he was quite certain that he knew everything there was to know about breeding rabbits and could not be manipulated by simple Leporids. It was perfect.

Josephine explained that if he could answer a simple riddle correctly, we would willingly and immediately enter into our reproductive obligation and attempt to produce hybrid offspring. But, if he was unable to answer correctly, he must grant me limited freedom (I promised not to run away) and construct a system permitting me access to her hutch in daylight hours for the same reproductive end. He agreed, and I am sure he thought that, regardless of the outcome, it would be a win for him and his liger rabbits were as good as in his hands. I insisted that he present his solution in 24 hours and there could be no outside help.

I put the problem to him as simply as I could and counted on human arrogance to assure him that he could not possibly be outsmarted by a wild jack rabbit. The riddle was presented in this form: 1) mature rabbit pairs reproduce a single pair of immature rabbits each month; 2) immature pairs reach sexual maturity after one month; 3) we begin with a single immature pair and ask how many pairs will there be at the end of 12 months of reproduction, assuming no deaths in the population?

The master wrote out the riddle in his breeder's note book and made me repeat it three times before he was satisfied. I think he suspected trickery. That evening, Josephine and I watched the light in his office window and it did not go off before three in the morning. I knew what to expect.

The next morning, a haggard master showed up in front of our cages with a wheel barrow transporting a six-foot-long, two-by-six-inch plank with five one-by-two-inch cleats nailed to it crosswise at one foot intervals. Josephine and I both wore our serious faces, we had humiliated our master and it was no time for gleeful celebration. Not yet, anyhow.

The master kneeled before my hutch and gave me a long and meaningful stare. At length he said to me "I don't know how you did it, but you did, and I am a man of my word, even to a pesky jack rabbit." With this he unlocked and opened the door of my cage and placed me on the ground. Then he opened Josephine's cage and leaned the cleated plank against the doorway. "There, I have complied with my part of our wager, now get your ass in there and start making babies."

I actually had to bite my lip to maintain my composure because I knew he would be asking me one more question. The villainous Uncle Dickie could not follow any of our conversation but he could understand the implications of my release and the plank leading into Josephine's cage. He began frantically sprinting around the restricted perimeter of his lodging at high speed, clacking his incisors and frothing at the mouth. I was positive that he had gone berserk, but it was only a manic expression of jealous rage and subsided quickly to an incredible torrent of steaming pellets and hateful glares at both me and the master, who ignored his tantrum entirely.

The master snatched me off the ground and carried me to a table under a shade tree at some distance from the rabbit population. Sitting on my haunches, we were eye-to-eye and, in my mind at least, speaking as equals. He said pointedly "You *must* show me how to solve this damned, baffling riddle before I go crazy. I spent hours on the blasted thing and could not get past month three with three rabbit pairs."

"Yes" I said, "the problem is, perhaps, a bit more difficult than it appears; it can be solved graphically by drawing different symbols for mature and immature pairs for each passing month but this becomes a rather tedious process when you get past six months. The key thing is to understand that the reproductive scheme generates a number sequence in which each term is the sum of the two preceding terms. Starting with pair 1, the next term is also 1 because it is the sum of 0 + 1, then one can construct the entire sequence easily and quickly as 1, 1, 2, 3, 5, 8, 13, 21, 34, 55, 89, 144, 233, and so on. This is the famed Fibonacci number sequence, first published in the year 1202. The first 1 records the initial, immature pair and the second 1 records this same pair at sexual maturity one month later. So the 13th term in the series is the number 233 which records the total number of pairs after the elapse of one month, required for maturation of the initial pair, followed by 12 months of procreation."

"Yes, yes, I see it now" he exclaimed "and I clearly see that I have underestimated your intelligence. I did not expect such complications from a wild hare. You are an amazing animal! Do you know that I could make a fortune by taking you on the road and having you solve math problems in public?"

"I doubt that, master. I speak to you now, voluntarily, but I love Josephine and wish only to remain here, with her, under the conditions of our agreement. I absolutely refuse to become a travelling shill in your employ. But, I think our arrangement will displease the esteemed Uncle Dickie, so, perhaps, a sedative is in order for him. What do you think?" The master looked at me, winked, and gave me a broad smile.

All is now running smoothly at the Acme Rabbitry in Burnt Corn, Alabama and no hybrids were ever produced by my union with Miss Josie. This is for the best. We have proven that love and happiness are, in fact, possible between a hare and rabbit. Eventually, even the humiliated Uncle Dickie came to accept the exclusive mating between Miss Josie and myself, and this, with only limited invective and without his nasty nocturnal soliloquies.

A BIRD OF CONSTANT SORROW

Yes, it is true, I am a bird of constant sorrow. I am a broken-hearted cardinal, not one of those Vatican guys with red beanies or a baseball player, but the avian kind known as *Cardinalis cardinalis*. Males, like myself, are bright, glossy red and, in fact, we are the only entirely red bird in North America. Did you know that? We are nervous, territorial birds often seen flitting between branches and issuing our melodious calls. If you have a bird feeder, you will see male cardinals in combat to control access to those delicious seeds. We are seed-eaters, you know, and we especially love sunflower seeds; for this reason, we do not migrate like insect-eaters and you have the pleasure of seeing us during your winter months unless you live someplace like Caribou, Maine where it is too cold for even rocks to survive.

No doubt you are surprised to read an account composed by a small red bird but there is no call for alarm. I have a literary agent and that makes all things, even idiomatic English, possible. She is quite taken with the idea of a bird writing tragedy, as if the lives of birds were all play, copulation and song. My sadness and consequent degradation is due to the loss of my dear mate, Adriana, and I want to tell you my story.

Our mating season began in mid-March and I arrived at our nesting site of the previous year exactly on March 15th, but Adriana did not. I called unceasingly for five days until I could call no more and attracted only one wicked male mocking bird, a disgusting fellow. You should know that mocking birds are the most useless creatures in the animal kingdom and only fit for cat food. Their pitiful imitation of cardinal calls is hysterically off-key and amounts to gibberish in our musical language. Our call, while it cannot be transliterated into English, is a clear, three-note whistle in declining pitch that goes something like *whoit-whoit-whoit*. While on the subject of dislikes, I should mention that cardinals hate brown-headed catbirds who habitually invade our nests to substitute one of their odious spotted eggs for one of ours. By substitute, I mean the female catbird eats one, or more, of our eggs and leaves hers in their place, forcing responsibility for her young onto hard-working cardinals. It is a parasitic form of socialism that no self-respecting cardinal can abide. Most people are surprised to learn that we do not like robins. Yes, I know they are cute with their bob-bob-bobbing in your back yard but they are insectivores; they actually eat worms! Slimy, gritty, wiggly things without eyes; we never consider inviting robins as dinner guests, nor should you. There are other dislikes, nasty boys with BB guns, your Easter bunny-egg myth, but these are universal among birds.

I must apologize, I have strayed from my story of Adriana, but mocking birds and catbirds always set me off in a fit of anger. The thing is, that normally, cardinals are socially monogamous, meaning we mate for life. At least, that is what bird books say, but I must warn the reader that this must not be taken too literally. As we say, "birds are birds" and a certain amount of promiscuity and extra-pair fornication is not unheard of. This would involve certain lower-class individuals, but certainly not Adriana and myself; yes, even cardinal society is guilty of social stratification.

However, after failing to meet Adriana, I began to think that, perhaps, she had died during the winter which was severe. I mention this possibility only because our median life span is three years and normal distributions being what they are, some individuals naturally expire sooner and some later. I knew Adriana was a two-year-old when we mated last year, so death was a statistical possibility and would mean that I should be open to looking for a new mate. I, myself, am in my third year but am quite hale and hearty and expect to be able to make fledglings for at least two more seasons, maybe more.

After exhausting myself calling, I finally recalled that I had seen Adriana on two occasions during the previous June after our second brood of fledglings took to the sky. On each of these sightings she was perched in a red mulberry tree frequented by un-mated birds, widows, widowers, and individuals of low degree. You should know that red mulberry trees are the bane of all bird species, including cardinals. They are analogous to neighborhood bars in your larger cities. This is because the purple fruits appearing on these trees between April and June have a high sugar content which ferments in warm weather. The consequence of this is that birds eating such fruit become quite drunk and, as with humans, this leads to poor decisions and promiscuous conduct.

This train of thought forced me to consider the unpleasant

possibility that my beloved Adriana may have become a red mulberry habitué, or in your terms, a barfly, the lowest rung on our social ladder. When birds get too drunk to eat berries from a perch in the tree, they resort to eating fallen fruit off the ground where they are easy prey for cats and BB guns. Disgraceful! But, perhaps parting with our dear nestlings, which is the only acceptable action for cardinals, somehow muddled her mind and turned her to mulberry juice. It seemed out of character, but still possible. Most mulberry addicts completely give up the acts of mating and reproduction and devote themselves fully and completely to the insidious berry. Could this be the explanation for my loneliness? I had only to fly to the iniquitous tree to find out.

As I contemplated my next move, a female cardinal dropped down on a branch close enough to suggest sexual interest but far enough to preserve modesty. I examined her physical attributes in comparison to Adriana; she was older, perhaps four years of age, her beak and plumage were acceptable though of slightly lower quality than one might wish for. I did admire the bright, active, coquettish expression in her eyes, though this betrayed her age in a droll way, like an overly mature actress cast in one too many leading roles. Countering these negatives were my own immediate needs, which weighed heavily, remember it had been a whole year; of course, I was also driven by the timeless genetic imperative to reproduce more cardinals. Consequently, I decided to woo this female, in spite of the enumerated reservations, and began my courtship routine.

Perhaps you would care to know the details of our mating rituals, they are rather intricate and, I think, should be interesting to humans. It revolves around the appearance and dancing skills of the male bird; his beak and plumage must be glossy red, the head crest full and upright and the black face mask large, but not clownishly so. We male cardinals have a saying "No glow, no go" meaning that dull or wilting plumage, or premature molting, suggests poor health and no female can accept that.

So when an attractive female comes within range, the male initiates a formal courtship-display by alighting on the ground and drooping his wings, fanning his tail and rocking. He must have a large seed, of high quality, in his beak when this ritual begins. If his overtures are greeted with success, the female will accept the seed, take it from the male's beak and eat it. That's it, the courtship is concluded and the individuals are mated and may copulate publicly without shame or censure. It sounds simple enough, but there must be art in the presentation or it will be rejected and that happens sometimes. Not to me, of course, there is nothing wrong with my beak, crest or plumage and I can dance with the best.

There was no need to give this performance more gusto than the required minimum as I knew the lady, whose name turned out to Sabine, would accept my advances. Afterward, she assured me that she was an excellent nest-builder and brooder and would work hard to make our breeding effort a success. I am sure she was thinking that this season would be her last as a mother.

So, I was re-mated, discharged the requisite copulatory duties, and began gathering materials for nesting while Sabine selected the site for our efforts and began construction. All of this was in absolute compliance with the cardinal code of good conduct but, from the male bird's perspective, this did not guarantee that all will go smoothly. I refer to rare cases where the first mate shows up after the male has taken a second. Try to imagine the disruption that follows. While one female is assiduously constructing the nest, the other, with equal determination, is bent on destroying it. There is much bad language exchanged, pecking and wing flapping; if there are eggs in the nest they are invariably broken or thrown to the ground.

The male bird must stand by helplessly and watch this squabbling until one female is defeated and leaves in humiliation, perhaps to join the unsavory revelries in the nearest mulberry tree. One might think this would close the issue, but often it does not, because the defeated lady may return in a drunken state for additional combat. Such chaos might continue over several days, breaking eggs and delaying the hatching schedule and contributes nothing to the reproductive plan. But, the worst of it is that the nest location is revealed to all birds, cats and boys in the neighborhood. Fortunately, this did not happen, but Adriana did make an appearance at my new nest site, and she was drunk.

Once the nest is constructed, the female lays three or four eggs and brooding begins. She does this alone, the incubation period being 12 or 13 days; during this period the male brings her food and zealously guards the area around the tree from inquisitive intruders. When the hatchlings emerge, the male must bring food for them, as well as for the female. Many people are surprised by the fact that male chicks are not adorned with royal red plumage when they fledge. It is true, they will not achieve this distinction until the following winter when they are ready for sexual activity. The nest is most vulnerable during this hatchling period as the male must be on foraging missions much of the time. This vulnerability lasts until the young are fledged and ready to fly down from the nest, about ten days after hatch. However, the male must continue to feed the fledglings and teach them foraging skills. Meanwhile, his mate will build a second nest, near the first, and lay another clutch of eggs. If there is need, such as a cat at the foot of the tree or the appearance of a female catbird, the lady cardinal has a special call that will summon her mate immediately to deal with danger.

The final day that I shared with Sabine was filled with pathos. The last of our progeny had taken wing and were no longer ours to teach and protect. This is the way with birds, no lingering familial kinships, no painful goodbyes, just a quick flight around the nest tree, and off toward the horizon. In a week they would not recognize their parents, nor we them.

Our breeding season was a complete success, we had reared six chicks without a loss, taught them to forage, and sent them skyward. The job cannot be done better. Still, I sensed a growing sadness in Sabine as this normally happy day approached. It was now time for the mated pair to part and I praised her hard work and mother-skills and encouraged her to meet me next March in this very tree. I am sure we both knew this was unlikely, but we promised each other and she flew off, perhaps to a mulberry tree, I do not know. I never saw Sabine again.

I took a final look around the area of our exhausting month of labor. As a male, in his prime, I basked in self-congratulatory exultation upon my parenting skills and speculated on what the next year might bring. I certainly anticipated a repeat performance with, in all probability, a new mate. This self-glorification was interrupted by the call of a female cardinal from no great distance. This was odd, in as much as there is no reason for cardinals of the opposite sex to communicate after the breeding season closes. This call was not strong but it was vaguely familiar. It was Adriana, beckoning me from the roof of a two-story house nearby. I flew to her, but afterward, wished I had not. She had aged so dramatically that she was almost unrecognizable; she was ungroomed, her crest wilted, her voice raspy, her beak was berry-stained and she was missing two wing feathers. She presented a picture of dissipation, an epitome of the ravages of alcohol and I wondered how she could fly in her condition.

Adriana apologized profusely for breaking our mate-ship. But it was as I suspected, her heart had been broken when our fledglings of last year flew away. She told me that, in the wake of this trauma, she had taken a vow of chastity, later modified to a vow of non-motherhood, which is not quite the same. I do hope readers realize that this extreme attachment to progeny is counter to law passed down through 10,000 generations of cardinals. It is anti-Darwinian, un-birdlike, unpardonable.

This *mea culpa* was presented with much weeping and with less coherence than I have used to convey it to you but, at the end of it, of course, I assured her of my forgiveness and wished her well. In truth, I could not forgive her outrageous conduct, but I did wish to conclude this wretched interview and get on with my life. I was not that lucky. Adriana insisted on knowing every detail about Sabine, her nest-building method, her brooding technique, and her mating skills, everything. Before it was over I wanted to drown myself in a vat of mulberry juice. Eventually, the call of the berry became too much and she muttered another pathetic apology and took off on unsteady wings for her refuge from regrets.

I remained in the vicinity of the nesting tree, visiting it often, and feeding voraciously on a good variety of seeds offered by neighborhood bird feeders. This was necessary to rebuild my strength and gain back weight lost to the rigors of reproduction. During this recuperative period, I had much time for contemplation and thought often of Adriana and her situation.

I hate to use the word *pity* because it hardly exists in the vocabulary of cardinals, or the animal kingdom in general. This emotion is not conducive to procreation and, as the case of Adriana demonstrates, can be antithetic. Everyone understands that evolution, and its well- known corollaries, are pitiless when it comes to mutant individuals. Yet, I began thinking of Adriana in less harsh terms, which is simply saying that I began to pity the poor lady. I could see no reason to condemn her for loving our young beyond the limits prescribed by cardinal law. I was aware that she could not live much longer on her present course and resolved to find her and do what I could to moderate her life style. It should be clear to anyone that I had no experience with berry addicts.

It was not difficult to find Adriana's mulberry tree. It was late afternoon and rollicking, drunken birds were rolling and twitching on the ground, interspecies sex was rampant, and mocking birds were orchestrating the debauchery. I observed these unholy proceedings from a nearby tree, hoping to see Adriana without actually entering into the pandemonium before me. At length, a tipsy robin landed in my tree and I inquired about Adriana, giving him a description of the lady. Yes, he knew her, but she had not been to the tree in several days and there was rumor that she had died. Dead? Could it be true? Was I too late? I was barely able to hold my perch. A wave of regret and heart-wrenching pain swept over me and I returned to my nesting tree to digest these tragic tidings. I resolved to revisit the mulberry tree in the early morning when some semi-sober birds might be found. This was a fatal decision.

The following morning, I appeared at the tree of disgrace and interviewed several early arrivals. They confirmed what the tipsy robin had told me, Adriana was dead. I had prepared myself for this, but still it propelled me into a vortex of depression and, before I realized what was happening, I had eaten one of the forbidden fruits. The effect was immediate and life-altering, I was high for the first time in my life. I ate a second berry and became bellicose, initiating a scuffle with a mocking bird who thrashed me thoroughly and pulled out one of my beautiful tail feathers. You can guess the rest, I continued eating berries until I fell to the ground totally besotted. When I regained consciousness, my newly acquired friends urged me to avoid the trials of hangover by "getting back in the saddle" and I did.

So now, I am a berry addict, I never leave the tree, I think no more of sex and reproduction, my weight is half its healthy value, and my beautiful, glossy, red plumage is a disgrace. I know my fate is to be eaten by a cat and do not care. He is welcome to my meatless, worthless bones. I am a broken and dissipated bird, a bird of constant sorrow.

GOOD MORNING LISBON

It was 6:15 a.m., clear and cloudless as the plane carrying Doc Martin, contract geologist, began circling Lisbon for descent. Martin loved this early morning vista of the old city when it was illuminated by the oblique rays of the red rising sun. The eastern sides of the mostly white buildings and their glowing red tile roofs contrasted wonderfully with the still-dark streets defining the labyrinthine skeleton of this historic city. Although he could not hear them, he knew that on this, as on every morning, countless city-dwelling roosters crowed their hearts out as sunlight reached their cages. It was a sound, that even in imagination, ushered him back through misty decades to his boyhood on a ranch in central Texas, and as always, recollection of that solitary lad and his simple life of fighting pirates and wild Comanches pierced his heart with the arrow of nostalgia for times and people long departed. It very nearly drew tears.

From his window seat, Doc Martin could discern the famed Praça Marquês de Pombal and the grand, 90-meter-wide Avenida da Liberdade running southeasterly one kilometer to the well-known Rossio business district and the train station. Unbidden, his mind's eye recalled warm summer evenings of drinking wine on Praça Dom Pedro IV in the Rossio with jovial companions bathed in the neon radiance of the eerie billboard featuring the mysterious, black-caped Don of Aguias promoting Sandeman port wine.

From the air, the Rio Tejo resembled a great reflecting platinum snake, as pristine as the upper Yukon River of eastern Alaska, but having seen the Tejo at close hand many times, Doc knew this was far from the case

This was not Doc Martin's first aerial view of Lisbon. That had come more than 20 years earlier when he was a professor at a major U.S. university on a year-long sabbatical leave at Portugal's prestigious Coimbra University. He was in his forties then, a bachelor and pure academic, concerned almost exclusively with publishing his research and attending conferences in exotic venues. These days he taught very little, and that was a gratis effort in a small, almost nameless college, in the dusty middle of Texas. Now, his income came from working periodically as a contract geologist for companies exploring the remote regions of the world for precious metals, tin and tungsten.

On this particular day, he was starting a new job for the Berault Tin and Tungsten Company and headed for the small city of Pinhão in north-eastern Portugal. He had been hired to evaluate several tungsten deposits in this area that were being considered for development by the company and its nexus of nameless partners.

His neighbor, living on the adjoining ranch outside of Llano, Texas, and his traveling companion on this day, was Senhora Modesta Gomez da Silva, a native born Portuguese from the village of Mealhada, located just north of Coimbra. Modesta had dark eyes, black hair with a few traces of grey, and olive skin darkened by exposure to the Texas sun. She had married Felice Gomez da Silva, also a native Portuguese, in Austin, Texas 15 years ago. With help from both of their families they had managed to purchase 640 acres adjacent to the Martin ranch ten years ago. She and Felice had two children, raised goats, and made a modest living from meat, milk, cheese, and breeding stock. Modesta had a degree in horticulture from the venerable Coimbra University and was very excited to be in back her native country to see her mother and father after a separation of four years. The Gomez da Silva family and the Martin family were not only ranch neighbors but close friends.

Martin guided the rented Land Rover out of the airport parking lot and onto the four-lane connecting Lisbon with Coimbra 200 kilometers to the north. He planned lunch in Coimbra and would then drop Modesta in the village of Meahada, an additional 20 kilometers north of Coimbra.

Modesta opened the conversation with "So, professor, how is it that you can make money from wolfram in rocks?" Modesta loved using the title of professor facetiously in her conversations with Doc Martin. "I remember my grandfather telling me he was a *wolframista* during the big war and made much money from the Germans, who paid in gold, but only for a short while. The deposit he worked on did not produce but for one year."

"Yes Modesta, many Portuguese farmers became *wolframistas* during the early years of World War II. Usually, they mined the mineral scheelite which is calcium tungstate, or $CaWO_4$. It was an easy matter to search out scheelite because it displays strong blue fluorescence under a black light in darkness. It was also easy to mine such ores, concentrate the scheelite by hand sorting and transport it by mules to German buyers in Vilar Formosa. The entire operation could be accomplished at night. But then, President Salazar nationalized Portugal's wolfram industry and set up severe penalties for those who engaged in such black market enterprises. After that, most of this activity stopped."

"But why did the Germans need our wolfram? Why could they not dig it out of their own rocks in Germany?" she asked with a quizzical look.

"Because they needed far, far more of this rare metal than Germany and Austria could ever provide. No country, not even the United States, is entirely self-sufficient in every mineral resource and war time brings on needs that political leaders, with their very limited fields of knowledge, do not anticipate. The Nazis bought all the wolfram that Spain could produce and all that Portugal would sell. Portugal's president, Salazar, dearly wanted to preserve Portugal's neutrality and colonial holdings, so he sold equal amounts of the metal to both the British and the Germans. Predictably, the Nazis encouraged Portuguese farmers to smuggle wolfram into Spain which upset this balance and pissed off the Brits in a major way."

"But why did my country sell anything to those evil Nazis? They were mean, ugly fellows, were they not?" she asked with her color rising. Modesta was 20 years younger than Doc and poorly informed on the subject of Portugal's role in WWII history.

"Yes Modesta, they were very bad guys but both Salazar and the Brits realized that the Nazis could invade Portugal and take all of the country's wolfram anytime they chose. Neither the British nor the Portuguese army were in a position to defend the country, so Salazar thought it better for Portugal to make money off the Germans rather than let them occupy the country as they did in Norway and Denmark."

"I see, professor. You are very smart to know these things. What was it that made wolfram so valuable to those bad Nazis?"

"Let me start, Modesta, by saying that the element wolfram is shown as W, element number 74, on the periodic table and is more commonly known as tungsten these days. Incidentally, wolfram has the highest melting point of any pure metal at 3422 degrees Celsius. When it is alloyed with carbon, you have tungsten carbide which rivals diamond in hardness and resistance to high temperatures, abrasion, and corrosion; when this compound is added to steel, it makes the steel suitable for high speed cutting tools, dies, ball bearings, luminous filaments, electrodes in park plugs, X-ray tubes, armor plating, armor-piercing ammunition, and turbine blades in rocket and jet engines. The German war industries needed all the tungsten it could get its hands on to make these things. Today, there are countless additional uses for this metal in metallurgy and chemistry. Why, surely you know that it is a very popular metal for men's wedding rings these days?"

"Yes, I have heard of such tungsten rings; they are shiny grey and rather handsome. But I did not connect tungsten with the name wolfram. Husbands like these rings better than gold because they do not deform when they work with their hands and their wives, of course, want their husbands to wear their rings to work."

They drove on in silence for a few minutes, passing through Leiria, with its well-known cathedral and castle, while Modesta digested this information and formulated her next question. Doc Martin estimated the remaining distance to Coimbra at about 90 kilometers which would put them in Coimbra in a little less than an hour.

"Okay professor, now I know something about why the Germans wanted our wolfram, so now please tell me about the role a geologist plays in this business. Why do they pay you to come to Portugal when I know we have our own geologists here?"

Doc laughed outright at this and finally answered "Why Modesta, they pay me for the same reason people in Llano pay you for your horticultural advice. I have worked on tin and tungsten ores in Alaska and Brazil for many years and this means that I know how to find deposits and estimate their grade and production potential on the current market. That is what they pay me for. I sell my knowledge and practical experience with certain minerals in the same way you do with plants."

"But Senhor professor, Alaska and Portugal are nothing alike in geography and climate. Does that not make a big problem for you?"

"No, Modesta, it doesn't" replied Doc with another laugh.

"There are really just two types of economic tungsten deposits; one of these features quartz veins and associated wolframite and cassiterite which produce tungsten and tin respectively. The famous mine at Panasqueira in central Portugal is of this type. The second type are scheelite replacement zones in limestones which are rather common in northern Portugal where I am heading tonight. At any rate, both types of deposits are found either at, or very close to, the margins of special types of granite bodies. This means that the geologist searching for tungsten deposits has to know a little something about granites. Climate, geography, latitude and that sort of thing play no role at all in determining where these special granites occur."

Modesta, now smiling, said "So, Doc, you are telling me that tungsten is like the azalea bush which cannot be found in alkaline soils with poor drainage."

"You have got it, Senhora Horticulturista."

"Ok, please now tell me how the wolfram gets out of the rock and into such things as light bulbs and wedding rings" she asked as the Land Rover approached the outskirts of Coimbra.

"Well, Modesta, this is essentially a problem in inorganic chemistry. You see, tungsten does not occur as a native metal like gold, silver or copper. It occurs as a chemical compound with oxygen and some other metals in the minerals wolframite and scheelite for the most part. Wolframite carries about 76 weight per cent WO_3 and scheelite has about 80 weight per cent WO_3. This compound, WO_3, is called tungsten trioxide and it is the money material in the rock as far as wolfram mining goes. Since most ore rocks being mined contains less than 2 per cent WO_3 by weight, and all of this is contained in the crystals of scheelite or wolframite, these minerals have to be separated from the 98 per cent of the rock that is considered waste. Concentrating the money stuff and getting rid of the waste in an efficient way is the job of the of the mills and extractive metallurgists. The mills produce 40 kilogram bags of either scheelite or wolframite concentrate in the form of powder and it generally runs about 75 weight per cent WO_3 because of minor impurities. The mill sells this concentrate to smelters and refiners and those guys convert it into chemical forms of tungsten wanted by different manufacturing industries. So, you can see that quite a few complicated things have to happen after a geologist finds the tungsten ore before one can buy that tungsten wedding ring."

"Yes, I can see that it must involve not only geologists and miners, but also mill workers, engineers, metallurgists, chemists, factory workers and ultimately jewelers. Thank you for this most entertaining lecture, professor. I never suspected how many people are required to make a wedding ring" replied Modesta, smiling broadly.

At this point they turned off the main highway into the narrow, congested streets of Coimbra. This old city dates back to Roman times and served as the capital city of Portugal between 1139 and 1256. Doc zigzagged through the streets of lower old town until he reached the northeast bank of the Rio Mondego and turned onto Avenida Emídio Navarro which follows the river along the base of the hill supporting many of the multi-storied, colonial, tile-roofed buildings of the university. This venerable seat of learning, founded in 1290, is Europe's second oldest university and boasts of a golden library, a 16th century Romanesque aqueduct, and beautiful botanical gardens established in 1772.

Both Doc and Modesta unconsciously glanced at the old university clock tower, the highest structure in the city of 144 thousand residents, and compared its reading with their wrist watches. This ancient hilltop timepiece, which controls the comings and goings of forty-thousand students and faculty, was right on the money.

At last, Doc aimed the Land Rover into the parking lot of the train station opposite the Hotel Bragança and said "Now Modesta, we'll park here and walk two short blocks to a restaurant that I used to go to often when I lived in Coimbra. I hope it is still open for business."

Doc Martin and Dona Modesta Gomez de Silva were seated in the Restaurante Rei Denis at a small table covered by a spotless, starched, white table cloth. Although Modesta had attended Coimbra University for four years which, in fact, overlapped Doc's sabbatical year, she was not familiar with this restaurant. University students could not afford the prices of Rei Denis.

A crackling cold bottle of white house wine and two glasses were placed between them as they surveyed the frenetic scene surrounding them. The dining room had rather low ceilings and less than perfect ventilation resulting in a distinctly smoky atmosphere produced by a wood-fired interior grill near the entrance door. The smell of roasted chicken, garlic and humanity permeated the room and floated at least 50 meters in all directions from the restaurant, beckoning additional diners. Half-a-dozen chefs sweated over spattering, spatchcocked chickens on the flaming grill while waiters in white dinner jackets and black bow ties snaked through the impossibly crowded dining room balancing overhead trays loaded with wine bottles and plates of sputtering chicken and rice. The din produced by 250, or so, happy diners conversing in unison competed against the clanking cacophony of kitchen noises. Add to this, the wood smoke, and the atmosphere of Rei Denis exactly replicated the rowdy chaos of a drunken medieval jousting festival.

Modesta leaned close to Marten's ear to exclaim "I love this place! It has everything we Portuguese love. Thank you so much for bringing me here."

"Maybe you should wait until we get our lunch before you praise it too much" Doc shouted back. They both laughed at the comedic situation. Their chicken and rice arrived just as the first bottle of wine expired and Doc ordered a second. It was always this way at Rei Denis and this is precisely why the diners in this worthy eatery are always happy and overly loud.

Doc looked into Modesta's dark eyes as he refilled her glass and his mind drifted back 20 years to another pair of similar dark eyes. Those of a woman he sat across from in this same restaurant.

Leticia was her name, Leticia Maria de Andrada, a beautiful professor of ornithology. They had fallen in love during his sabbatical year and talked of marriage. Things did not work out well, as both parties were unwilling to give up their academic positions. He did not think about Leticia often, at least not these days, but looking into Modesta's eyes brought it all back. Heartbreak can last a lifetime, that was one thing that Doc Martin knew for sure. Maybe this was the reason that he had never married during the decades since. Maybe.

An hour after leaving Rei Denis, the Land Rover pulled into the Mealhada farm yard of Modesta's parents, the place where she was born and raised. Chickens, ducks and geese scattered and squawked, quacked and hissed, while a resplendent male bronze turkey regally strutted and gobbled, and a large black dog of indefinite breed and formidable appearance attacked the car. The farmhouse itself, was white, tile-roofed, and its walls were covered by espaliered fruit trees that supported vigorously growing grape vines. All of this was quite in character for a traditional Portuguese *quinta*, or small farm.

Modesta's parents were out to the vehicle in a flash sending their dog away and hugging and kissing their daughter. They also hugged and kissed Martin, whom they had met some years before, but this kissing was in the more formal, traditional manner of rural Portuguese known as the *abraça*.

Doc pulled Modesta's suitcase out of the Land Rover and reminded her to telephone him in Pinhão where he planned to stay for, at least, the next two weeks. His plans included a return to Meahada to take Modesta and her parents to the Rei des Leitões restaurant, a place famous throughout Portugal for glazed roast pig, known as *leitão*, and their excellent cold *vinho verde* white wine.

Martin's planned departure did not please Modesta's parents who argued that he should stay for dinner and a night's rest before going on. With great effort, Doc was, at last, able to convince this worthy farm couple that his contract required him to be in Pinhão, 200 kilometers farther north, and at work early the next morning. Eventually he was allowed to depart in the Land Rover for Pinhão but, of course, this necessitated another round of mandatory *abraças*.

I, AGAVE

Do you like my title? It is intended it to elicit the pomposity and vanity of a Caesar but is, frankly, just an insecure writer's trick to gain attention. There is nothing Caesarian in this story but I do pass on one weak metaphor about Roman legions. Calling myself a writer is, perhaps, also misleading because I am, in fact, an agave, a simple green plant, chlorophyll, photosynthesis, oxygen waste and all the rest of that metabolic stuff found in botany textbooks. But really, wouldn't you like to know how the world looks from a plant's perspective? After all, don't green plants supply the oxygen that is so precious to your life? So, I say, suspend your disbelief momentarily and read on, you are bound to learn a thing or two about life and tequila.

Plants necessarily lead a sedentary life and, for this reason, they know all there is to know of soils and climates and tend to be rather more philosophical than the mobile creatures of the animal kingdom. Yes, I know, you think plants are mindless, soulless life forms, incapable of feeling, thought, or purpose and that our methods of reproduction, although classed as sexual by botanists, lacks the intimacy of vaginas and penises in your world. But restrain your arrogance and bear in mind that agaves are succulent, vascular plants that possess both male and female organs and, at maturity, can reproduce in a truly spectacular sexual manner.

Who does not stand in awe of the immense flowering-stalk of the century plant, *Agave americana*, covered in yellow florets and reaching skyward to heights of 30 feet. Did you know that this bizarre phallic structure emits a special musky odor that attracts bats from great distances? Bats are well known as the primary pollinators for agaves. Regrettably, it is also true that the agave plant dies after this dramatic sexual display, but what living organism does not die? Anyone with an agave in the backyard knows that asexual, vegetative reproduction by lateral shoots begins early in lives of agaves and is repeated many times before that great, fatal, sexual climax is reached. Humans call the plant producing such adventitious shoots the "mother plant", but why? In fact, it is no more of a mother than it is a father. It is silly.

Who would want to be a plant, you will ask, to be gobbled up by arrogant vegetarians, who extract virtue from exclusively dining on plants? Who wants to be digested by hungry cows only to be expelled as splattering feces? These are fair questions and I will answer them in due course. But first, I must explain a few elementary things that distinguish the genus Agave, with its 200 plus species, from other common plants and why it is that we consider ourselves as plant royalty, deserving of both pomposity and vanity.

Firstly, we are not cacti just because we have sharp spines and frightful barbs. There are so many differences between agaves and cacti that it is difficult to know where to begin. Let us dispense with the botanical taxonomy by simply saying that cacti and agaves are both angiosperms, that is, flowering, covered-seed plants that date back to Triassic times, perhaps as much as 250 million years. However, we differ at the class level, agaves being of the class monocotyledonae, whereas cacti are members of the class dicotyledonae. The nomenclature is formidable, is it not? That's botany for you, don't take up the study if big words frighten you.

The distinction between monocots and dicots is not restricted to the organs of embryonic development, which are known to all, but is manifest in a number of ways that do not require botanical expertise to appreciate. Monocot seeds are of one piece, dicot seeds easily split into two pieces like peanuts and the flowers of monocots display symmetry in multiples of three, whereas dicot flowers exhibit symmetry in multiples of four or five. If you need more, consider the venation of monocot leaves, the pattern of which is generally parallel the narrow, elongate length of the leave as in corn; in spikey dicot leaves the veins are reticulate, or net-patterned, as one sees in tomato plants, hickory trees and cacti. All monocots are herbaceous, including agaves, but dicots may be either herbaceous or woody. In short, they are very different types of plants, only distantly related, and are easily discriminated.

By now, esteemed reader, you are certainly asking yourself how a brainless, heartless, lungless plant could be telling a story of any kind, let alone one involving botanical distinctions. Plants cannot speak or write, obviously, so you will say this story is not credible. My answer is that plants are smarter than you think and that you must accept that some things are unknowable. For instance, why does an inner electron not fly into the positively charged nucleus of an atom to unite with a proton and be transformed to a neutron? Unknowable, is it not? Yet, you accept this model of the atom without objection. But, let us forego these dull questions of credibility and get on with my story. I promise it will be entertaining and it involves tequila.

So, I am a proud *Agave tequilana* Weber var. azul, the famed blue agave, from which the very best brands of tequila are derived. In fact, Mexican law prescribes that only this plant may be used in the process of making authentic tequilas. I reside in a central row on a very large agave plantation located close to the village named Tequila, some 60-kilometers northwest of Guadalajara, in the state of Jalisco, Mexico. Our mathematically straight rows are meticulously maintained through hand labor by men who are known as *jimadores*. Viewed from a distance, our geometric assemblage resembles that of Roman legions on parade. This, and the tequila thing, are the sources of our pride and vanity.

My particular plantation is owned and operated by the company known as *José Cuervo*, a name you are no doubt familiar with, perhaps overly so. The agave fields occupy large, flat valley floors surrounded by rugged mountains and are visited daily by thousands of human tourists packed into trains, busses and rental cars from Guadalajara. I assure you that we agaves know a lot about people and I will mention here that dog and human excrement is not beneficial to our soils or wellbeing. Stop fouling our beds, please.

All of the plants within range of my senses are exactly like me in size, color, conformation and age, which is ten years at this moment. We are selectively bred for uniformity which means individuality and deviation from the norm are traits frowned upon by our human masters. The masters are quite proud of this uniformity, but I must confess that I feel some degree of individuality in spite of the fact that I am physically indistinguishable from my companions. Collectively, my "brother" agaves and I are all of a slate-blue color, have about 250 leaves each, at present, and are rooted exactly two meters apart. At our present size, however, our leaves are sufficiently long to come into contact with those of our closest neighbors in the same row. I must admit that I love this social contact which allows a primitive, unspoken communion with those we touch. Those plants fortunate enough to occupy the end position of the long rows (sorry, I have no conception of this distance) are exposed to more of the world than we in central positions. When danger threatens, they act as sentinels and somehow, someway transfer their impressions along the row, agave to agave, through this touching to educate the entire community. Perhaps this is analogous to your universities. I only know that when the dangers of fire, drought, storm, or the approach of the hated harvesters or drunken tourists, occur, it is not long before our entire community of thousands is aware and on guard.

I hear you asking "how can brainless plants assume defensive action?" I am sure you know about the formidable spines at the ends of our leaves, everyone fears them, naturally. Well, it so happens that we can control the angle of our leaves to our axis of symmetry. This, of course, allows us to adjust the amount of sunlight we receive but there is more, much more related to this ability. When the leaves are tightly held in near-vertical position it preserves moisture during droughts, dust storms or wildfires and when they are relaxed to a nearly horizontal attitude they repel human or animal intruders and funnel rain to our roots. These defensive abilities surprise you, don't they?

I mentioned tequila earlier, and that is probably the only reason you are still reading my story. The process of making tequila is complex, as you might suspect, and from the agave perspective, it is a source of both pride and dread. I don't use the word fear, because I do not think that plants experience fear in the anticipatory sense of impending doom as people do. We are not obsessively concerned with the future as most humans are. Yes, plants mainly concern themselves with the present which brings enough difficulties for our taste and limited resources. Since agaves play the starring role in the tequila-making process you should not be surprised that we are well informed about the conversion of our body fluids to alcohol.

The steps in tequila production are closely regulated by the *Consejo Regulador de Tequila* and consist of harvesting, cooking, extraction, fermentation, distillation, aging and bottling. Of course, bottling is followed by consumption in the form of straight shots, prairie fires, and upside-down margaritas. But, clearly, these concoctions and the behavior they induce are not part of the manufacturing process.

Harvesting...if there is one euphemism that deserves eternal confinement in the fiery depths of hell, it is this word. It hides murder, and murder most foul. When agaves reach an age of about 12 years, our sugar content is at a peak and this is a fatal condition. The *jimadores*, wearing their protective shin-guards and leather aprons, come with their hellish *coas*, long-handled scythes resembling medieval halberds, and mercilessly dismember us by the thousands. Imagine the panic and consternation that passes up and down the rows of the peace-loving agaves. We cannot run, we cannot cry out, we cannot avoid the razor-sharp blades; we must wordlessly endure serial amputation of more than 250 of our precious life-giving limbs. You will, no doubt, ask if this is painful. Dear reader, are you stupid? Of course, it is painful, it is agonizing to be butchered alive in this uncivilized, piece-meal manner and, when all our leaves are severed, the unkindest cut of all is administered. This is the separation of our holy, living bole, weighing between 80 and 300 pounds, from our root system; the death blow, the *coup de grâce*, the end of life for an agave. The simple *jimadores* and the tequila industry are pleased to refer to this devilish act of betrayal as "removal of the *piña*", or heart, of the plant. Another euphemism worthy of Dante.

When the harvest of a field is complete, the view conjures the indelible victim photos of Hitler's holocaust. Thousands upon thousands of agave limbs are scattered about helter-skelter and *piñas* are stacked in appalling piles to be gathered by tractor-drawn trailers. Our leaves are left to mummify under the soulless Mexican sun even though the industry knows that our leaf fibers and pulp can be made into cordage, livestock feed, fertilizer, fabrics, paper and other useful items. No, they say, we are distillers of premium tequila, not makers of string, rope and household items. If you want a utility plant, then cultivate *Agave sisalana*, as they do in Brazil, but don't drink the awful liquor they make from it.

The horrifying element behind all this mindless harvesting carnage is the stark and dismal industrial equation: 15 pounds of *piñas* = 1 liter of tequila. Just think of it from our perspective. At the very least, I hope you will feel a tinge of guilt with that next margarita.

BUT, TODAY IS NOT HARVEST DAY FOR THE PLANTS THAT I LIVE AMONG, THAT DAY WILL COME SOON ENOUGH. WE HAVE ALWAYS KNOWN *THAT DAY* MUST COME. THE SIMPLE *PEÓNES* WHO CULTIVATE US ARE STILL OUR KINDLY CARETAKERS AND ARE NOT ARMED WITH THE WICKED, DEATH-DEALING *COAS* ON THIS DAY. BUT THERE IS NOT ONE OF US WHO WOULD NOT GIVE UP OUR PLACE IN THE ROW TO BE A WILD AGAVE, LIVING FREE IN THE ROUGH AND TUMBLE WORLD OF MOUNTAIN

DESERT PLANTS, DIVORCED FROM THE ILLUSTRIOUS DISTILLERY OF *JOSÉ CUERVO*, AND ORDAINED TO PRODUCE THAT GIANT, PHALLIC, FLOWER STALK THAT SPELLS BOTH BEGINNING AND END

CANTO DO VIRAPURU

Call me Moisés… but perhaps, you should know that my full name is Moisés Raimundo Nobres Chestymp and that I truly believe I was born under a brown star. This birth took place 30 years ago in Salvador, Bahia which lies on the coast of eastern Brazil. My Christian name is, of course, Portuguese for Moses but the origin of my surname is less certain. I have come to think it may be Welsh judging by the paucity of vowels, but there is no genealogical support for this. I can only say for certain that both my father and his father were native-born Brazilians. At any rate, my name is not important because I no longer exist, but this does not mean that I am dead, at least, not exactly. It does mean that there are fates worse than death and mine is an unholy example of what can happen when life and magic clash. Inasmuch as I have nothing more to lose, I may as well tell you my story. It starts with the song of a forest bird.

Canto do Virapuru … it has a wonderful, romantic, exotic sound, has it not? It translates as *song of the virapuru* which, of course, begs the question, what is a *virapuru*? *Virapuru* refers to an active bird in the wren-family celebrated in the folklore of Brazil. It is a real, but quite magical bird that dwells in the Amazon rain forest and confers life-long good luck in both love and business for any individual fortunate enough to hear it sing in the wild. This is not an easy feat by any means because this bird's calls are restricted to a few minutes at dawn and dusk during its mating season. This limits opportunities to about 15 days a year. The legends also claim that other forest birds are shamed into stony silence when the male *virapuru* begins his haunting song and this may be true.

Naturally, one must not expect to gain these same welcome benefits of the song by listening to recordings on the internet which anyone can do at any time. Still, by doing so, you can at least appreciate the moving, melodious, flute-like notes of this call which almost seems as if it were designed by some 19th century German or Italian master composer.

The word *virapuru* is synonymous with many alternative names for this legendary forest singer, including *Uirapuru-verdadeiro, Arapuru, Guirapuru* and others stemming from the *Tupí-Guaraní* word *wirapu'ru*. These names are usually transliterated to English as "musician bird" or "musician wren", which seem to me far less poetical and romantic than the Brazilian names. This multiplicity of titles should be considered a tribute to the enduring esteem Brazilians hold for this wonderful bird and the magical folklore surrounding it. This is also an excellent reminder of why we should treasure the system of binomial nomenclature devised by Linnaeus. In the case of *virapuru*, the Linnaean system reduces our quandary from *Tupí-Guaraní* words of uncertain meaning and impossible pronunciation to the staid, and more respectable, Latin *Cyphorhynus aradus*.

The male musician bird is adorned with a reddish-orange face, throat and chest with the remaining plumage being dark brown with thin white bars. Its legs are rather long and spindly with three toes forward and fourth in opposition to favor perching. The *virapuru* feeds on small insects, tropical fruits and, of course, the adoration of all Brazilians, rich or poor, young or old.

If you should be lucky enough to come into possession of a feather or nest fragment of this exalted bird, it would surely be equivalent to owning a piece of the True Cross or Shroud of Turin; it would mean that *Tupä*, chief god the of indigenous peoples of Brazil, will favor you, beyond all others, with wealth and loyal, passionate lovers.

Naturally, the phrase *"Canto do Virapuru"* is known by all who live in tropical Brazil and is consequently often appropriated to name fishing boats, city streets, hotels, restaurants and even bars. One such bar, my personal favorite, is located in the Brazilian city of Belém on Avenida Presidente Vargas at its intersection with Avenida Nazaré. This bar is situated directly across from the Praça República, a lovely green space in the heart of the city. It lies in the beating heart of the major bairro of Nazaré, only a few steps from the five-star Hilton Hotel, the city's finest. This bairro is the nexus of the city where financial business of all kinds is conducted during daylight hours and business of quite a different sort is transacted during nocturnal hours, which is just to say that this area is busy around the clock and is quite representative of central districts of all major South American cities.

So, permit me now to tell you a little of what life is like in

Belém. The work day starts early, about three a.m., when neighborhood panificadoras begin their work of making bread but this does not disrupt the sleeping city perceptibly because bakers are inconspicuous individuals and always live close to their ovens.

The real movement in the city begins in earnest about five a.m., slowly at first, but with rapidly increasing momentum. Buses head to the outlying bairros of the poor from twenty different bus terminals to bring thousands of cooks, maids, laundresses and gardeners into the city to serve the wealthy. The result is that the narrow streets of this old city are choked with these buses and their horrible diesel fumes permeate the atmosphere which, otherwise, would reek of decaying fruit, rotting fish and human excrement. It will be raining. It always seems to be raining in this crumbling colonial city.

Within the hour, the tropical sun will rise up from the Atlantic and streets will bustle with pedestrians, tradesmen, students, street hawkers, beggars, policemen, newspaper boys, two-wheeled donkey carts and street sweepers armed with palm branches; all of these worthy citizens are ready to begin their day. Conversely, drunks, gamblers, night watchmen, prostitutes and other creatures of the night will be returning to their homes after a long, wearying and, often, wet night.

If you are in the middle of the city, the musical accompaniment for this morning vignette is provided by insanely honking automobiles and taxis that capriciously ignore rules of the road and the leonine roar of dueling buses racing one another along the narrow streets to scoop up waiting passengers. These buses are entered from the rear door and exited from the front but actually only stop their forward progress if the prospective passenger appears to be over the age of sixty or is encumbered with a struggling live turkey or similar bulky, squirming burden. Youthful patrons are expected to board or exit on the move; there is no time to lose for drivers paid by the number of passengers entering the rear door.

But, perhaps, you are lucky enough to be near the edge of the city, close to the forest, where there will be considerably less noise. Here, you might be treated to the sight of a chattering troop of wild monkeys raiding garbage piles or, maybe, the disharmonic shrieking of a thousand gregarious, colorful parakeets roosting in a single tree as the sun rises.

These colorful, but fleeting, early morning minutes are the autumnal glory of the tropics, as cool and innervating as it ever gets, and it will end before nine a.m. unless it is cloudy and raining. This is Belém, founded by the Portuguese in 1616 at the gigantic mouth of the Amazon River, a mere 100 miles south of the equator.

The climate here is classed as tropical-wet; this means it is always hot and humid and there is no dry season, no cold season and 114 inches of rain in a year. It also means that the tall modern apartment buildings confined to the central district of Nazaré are disfigured by black mold no matter how recently they were painted and the 19th century sewer system is backed up in the lower parts of the city because it is hopelessly inadequate to serve the 1.5 million current residents.

The same could be said of the electrical system of the city which is subject to frequent, unpredictable losses of power described by the patiently-enduring citizens as *"falta de luz"*. Just imagine yourself confined in a coffin-sized apartment elevator with four other people for two hours waiting for restoration of electric current in *this* climate.

Running water is also the slave of electrical power because water pressure throughout the city is provided by gravity from rooftop cisterns which are replenished by electrical pumps. The result is that, even large modern air-conditioned buildings with running water will soon become quite unpleasant if electric power is lost for more than two hours. Toilets do not flush when their water supply is cut off.

So, it should be obvious to any reader why tourists are repelled by this city; it is dirty and noisy, the pervasive odors of tropical life are repulsive, the rain is miserable and the sun and humidity, the sole alternative, is oppressive. Add to this the unspeakable poverty, hardship and tropical diseases that greet one at every turn, and do not forget the nocturnal hordes of scrambling rats and crime enough for anyone's taste. Barred doors and windows and defensive walls, topped with broken glass to repel burglars, are a nearly universal feature in the inner parts of the city where the wealthy live. Thus, it cannot come as a surprise that even native Brazilians from the south, which is very European in climate and social outlook, say they hate Belém.

Of course you are asking yourself why would anyone want to live in this city or even visit. In a word, *commerce*. This is the thing that draws in outsiders; there is quite a large university, an excellent airport, world class port facilities, and of course, the Amazon River and its many large navigable tributaries that supply the world with a wealth of commodities from the tropics. Beyond the venerable colonial history and beautiful cathedrals of the city, you will find excellent churrascarias, weird but delightful indigenous dishes, a Carnival celebration that rivals any in Brazil and the world famous Círio celebration that annually overwhelms Nazaré with a tsunami of religious fervor favored by the Catholic church. But, even more important, are the cattle, aluminum, iron, gold, forest products which include timber, rubber and coffee; then there is leather, fish, all manner of tropical fruits, black pepper, açaí, guarana, dende oil, cacao, cashews, Brazil nuts and a few hundred other tropical items that pass through Belém to the outside world on a daily basis.

I suppose everyone knows about Salvador, my birth city, and its porridge of racial and cultural influences, its armies of topless female samba bands during Carnival, its sinful nightlife, religious syncretism and exquisite West African cuisine. Add to this, music, dancing, voodoo, history, famous writers like Jorge Amado, All Saints Bay, mystic lighthouses, beautiful colonial architecture and you have a real city, one well worth knowing.

I am almost ashamed to tell you that these colorful pursuits, that draw tourists from distant parts of the world, did not play much of a role in my early rearing. I was, from earliest years, drawn to books and learning from private tutors hired by my conservative, educated parents. It seems that I was destined to become an academic from the beginning and my life of learning passed uneventfully, even through my eight years of study at the Federal University of Bahia, where I was honored to receive a doctorate in the area of structural geology and rock mechanics. This degree was what led me to the city of Belém.

The Federal University of Pará, located in Belém, needed a man to teach rock mechanics to post-graduate students and I landed this position and left my home and parents in Salvador for the tropics in the north. My mother was horrified, of course, my father did not express an opinion but secretly harbored the thought that exposure to all those things not found in text books would prove to be a good thing for young Moisés. I can now say with certitude that he was wrong in this.

It required a few weeks to adapt to my new surroundings. I found an acceptable apartment in central Nazaré, learned to use the buses to get to the university located in the distant bairro of Guamá, and established friendships with my faculty colleagues and graduate students. I even grew accustomed to the Paraensé accent and slang which is rather different from the Portuguese employed in southern Brazil. I cannot claim that I ever came to appreciate the climate of the place.

I mentioned the bar called *Canto do Virapuru* as a favorite.

This is because it is the only bar in Belém that serves *cerveja do barril*, or draft beer, and as such, is extremely popular with college men and younger faculty from the university. On Friday and Saturday nights, in particular, the place is always crowded with never less than 250 to 300 boisterous, mostly male customers pouring dented metal flagons of beer down thirsty throats.

I, myself, am not much of a drinker but I enjoyed the noisy, raucous atmosphere and was always amused by the drunken antics of this happy crowd. I was totally astounded by the quantity of beer these college boys could consume and still maintain some degree of motor coordination. I have seen celebrating patrons enter the bar mounted on saddle horses, enveloped by large squirming boa constrictors, and once a fellow came in leading a giant ant-eater on a rope; all this to general applause, of course. Small Brocket deer, monkeys, juvenile alligators and parrots of various types, somehow pilfered from street venders, are commonly seen scampering, swinging, slithering and flying freely throughout the bar adding mirthful hilarity to the proceedings.

Obviously, the bar management is very tolerant of these pranks, makes peace with the street vendors the next day, and absorbs the resulting damages; city police never make an appearance, even during the wildest escapades, so I assume they are remunerated in some manner. Given this menu of jocose activities, I would not be surprised if you would place the *Canto do Virapuru* on your venue for a Saturday night of fun, that is, if you happened to be in Belém.

But there is more, and it has nothing to do with the hilarious revelry within this unique public establishment. At its entrance, on the sidewalk of Avenida Presidente Vargas, during the hours between 9 a.m. and 5 p.m., is stationed a beggar man, a mendicant of demonic aspect who lies at the center of this story.

He is a small man, though it is difficult to make this judgment because he has neither arms nor legs, only short stumps. For this reason, he is known as "*O Torse*", the torso, or sometimes "*O Fantoche*", the marionette. He is definitely a living entity, neither dwarf nor midget, but simply a very small, limbless, pitiful creature who appears to be deserving of public charity which he collects in a can placed in front of him. Stationed nearby are an inconspicuous attendant and body guard who provide transport, an umbrella and protection as needed.

Over the head of this grotesque individual and suspended in two closely spaced cages, sit two captive *virapuru* birds, a male and a female. They can see each other clearly but are physically restrained from mating or coming into contact, no doubt in the hope of eliciting the famous good-fortune call of the male. So far as any of the bar patrons know, and I have inquired widely, no one has ever heard a single note exchanged between these prisoner birds. They do not seem happy to be part of this supplicatory staging.

It cannot be said that *O Torse* stands, exactly, I do not think that is possible given his circumstances. Rather, he leans back in a slanting posture against a plywood structure which is supported by wooden braces configured in the geometry of the 3-4-5 right triangle of classical trigonometry. Such triangles are known as Pythagorean triples and exhibit integer sides in arithmetic progression and integer areas as well. I mention these mathematical details because I am rather proud of my knowledge in this field and it is obvious that whoever constructed this apparatus for *O Torse* is also well versed in trigonometry. At any rate, the result is that this diminutive beggar reclines from the vertical at an angle of precisely 36.87 degrees, an angle calculated to permit his eyes to meet those of innocently strolling pedestrians very directly, and I do mean *directly*.

I must attempt to describe my first encounter with this individual but I doubt my capacity to do so in a manner that allows the reader to fully grasp the horror that his face conveys to the observer. This face is hairless and rather small, of course, but not wrinkled, warty, scarred or ugly in any conventional way. The nose is regular, the mouth presents a tight, knowing, but sardonic, smile that I associate with long-held, captive monkeys. This shit-eating smile is the only expression this face ever exhibits. I suppose the creature speaks but confess that I have never heard a word pass his lips. His hair is black and cut short, the skin healthy and coppery in color, indicating indigenous blood, and quite the normal tone for this part of the world.

The face is youthful in a sense, not abnormal in any overt physical way but for the eyes; those damnable eyes… they are the deepest black I have ever seen in man or beast and so reflective that it seems you are looking into a mirror. You can easily see yourself in these reptilian orbs and it induces horror and vertigo in the observer. At least that was my impression when I stooped to place a coin in his collection can and our eyes met for an instant. His eyes were palpably evil, positively inhuman, monstrous. I felt like a shuddering, defenseless bird under the relentless, hooded gaze of Kipling's Nag-the-cobra and I knew instantly that I was staring into the eyes of Lucifer's spawn. I need not say that I disengaged from this unholy exchange abruptly and resolved never to approach this wicked creature again.

My resolution held for nearly a year, causing me to walk on the farther side of Presidente Vargas and enter the bar from a little-used alley entrance on the rare occasions when I visited before 5 p.m. It was a worthwhile inconvenience to avoid those hideous, implacable eyes at close range but *O Torse* always seemed to be aware of my presence during these skirting maneuvers and never failed to present me with his hideous, shit-eating, monkey smile. Naturally, I did not acknowledge this obscene gesture.

During this period of avoidance, which I would now classify as one of stalemate, I became aware of a faint, smoky-grey nimbus enveloping the head of this fearsome freak of nature; it was perceivable only at a distance and only at certain sun angles and disappeared entirely as one approached this unclean limbless thing. None of my acquaintances would confess to seeing this evil hood, but I knew it existed, and I am quite sure that *O Torse* knew that I knew. At any rate, I interpreted this loathsome optical effect as a malignant and demonic sign of the first order and renewed my vow to avoid eye contact with this diminutive creature of the streets.

The trouble began with an event at the university which is reckoned as the highest and gayest celebration in the academic world, the conferring of the degree of Doctor of Philosophy, the coveted Ph. D. The recipient was my first student to achieve this honor and I was extremely proud of him and his dissertation work.

Custom demanded that all post-graduate students, faculty and staff in the Geology Department attend the defense of the dissertation and the traditional party that followed. Music, food, wine, beer and cachaça were in abundance and all serious activities in the department were cancelled for the remainder of this special day. All attendees, the new Ph.D. in particular, were expected to get drunk and be taken home by their spouses when the festivities concluded. But, if things had followed this plan, I would not be telling you this story.

The honoree was quite drunk, of course, and I must admit that I was more than a little drunk myself when the ill-advised idea to adjourn to the *Canto do Virapuru* swept the room. Taxis were summoned, drunken academics piled in, and soon we were on Avenida Presidente Vargas at the front door of the bar at 3:30 p.m. With the support of two students, I was guided toward the front door along a trajectory that placed me directly before the limbless beggar. His permanent smile widened perceptibly and his eyes positively blazed like lasers into mine. Instantly, I became nauseous from intense vertigo and the last thing I remember seeing was the sidewalk rushing up to my face…and, oddly, I could plainly hear the lovely notes of the caged male *virapuru*.

I have no idea how long I was out of consciousness but when I opened my eyes again it was to see familiar eyes set in a familiar face. I was looking into my own eyes, or perhaps I should say, eyes that were formerly mine. I watched in dumb disbelief as my drunken friends carried an unsteady body that was mine into the revelry taking place behind the doors of the *Canto do Virapuru.*

I would suppose, that like me, you have not had much need for erudite terms like transfiguration, metamorphosis, metempsychosis, revenant, revivification or transmogrification; these self-indulgent words are only tossed about by conceited literary folks to lend an aura of pseudoscientific reality to their silly fiction. For a man of science, it is simply impossible to grasp such frivolous, unsupportable notions and yet…and yet, I now find myself leaning back on the 3-4-5 triangular contraption and looking sorrowfully and pathetically up into the eyes of passers-by on Avenida Presidente Vargas.

I dare say you will want to know the results of hearing the song of the *virapuru* bird. It all came true, just as the legend promises, and today, I am rewarded with wealth and a loyal passionate lover. But, this truth manifests itself in a grotesquely ironic way, a literal, yet horribly dissatisfying way.

As the front man for a begging syndicate, which in truth, is simply a criminal enterprise, I am quite wealthy by any measure, I eat very well indeed and my people will purchase any thing I wish.

But what is the value of wealth when all I wish for is my former body, or almost anyone's body, but not this limbless, monstrous thing they call *O Torse*? My people change my diaper twice a day (humiliating is it not?) but will not buy me prosthetic limbs because it would destroy the syndicate and their prosperous livelihood. Evidently, a bowl of rice and beans trumps all other considerations, including that for my soul.

As far as the loyal lover is concerned, this also comes with bitter irony. I have a woman, both attractive and loyal, who comes to bathe me nightly. Whenever I wish, she satisfies my, let us call them baroque, needs. But, of course, I am not describing emotional love or even affection here. This lady is member of the syndicate and her loyalty is to that body, certainly not to mine which is surely repulsive to her.

I know I should curse the magical *virapuru* bird, but I live with the knowledge that, what has happened once, can surely happen again, this is the founding pillar of geological science after all. So, I patiently await *you* beneath the cages confining the musician wrens at the front entrance of the bar *Canto do Virapuru*.

THREE SUNS ON THE HORIZON

2500-miles, that is almost the exact driving distance from Seattle, Washington to Coldfoot, Alaska and the first leg of a bucket-list adventure north of the Arctic Circle for two old geologists. Both of these worthies were teetering on the doorstep of retirement after nearly 50 years of productive employment for each. I arrived at the Seattle airport at about 10 a.m. local time, from Dallas, and found my old buddy from grad school days waiting with a big smile on his face.

It was August 31, 2014, I was 72 at the time, my host was 74, and we were eager to begin a long-planned caribou hunt north of the Arctic Circle, in the Brooks Range of northern Alaska. My friend, Reuben, had flown into Seattle two days earlier from Santiago, Chile, where he works as an independent consulting geologist nine months of the year. He and his Vietnamese wife, Kim, maintain their residence in Seattle, so this was our point of departure.

My career as a geologist was, more or less, finished when I retired from a university teaching position in January of 2013, although I did manage to pick up a part-time consulting job with a major mining company that lasted about a year. Now, that was over, and it seemed like I was an old fart on a lee shore as far as future employment went and the outlook for my friend was not much brighter. It seemed a waste that our one hundred years of combined international experience was headed for the toilet.

We had lunch at a Vietnamese restaurant owned by one of Reuben's brothers-in-law, but were not allowed to pay, so Reuben slyly deposited a twenty in the tip jar on the counter next to the cash register. Next, we drove to a Cabela's store located on the outskirts of Seattle and purchased a good deal of personal equipment that could not be accommodated on commercial airlines. I bought an expensive air mattress, two rubber duffle bags, and a liner for my sleeping bag while Reuben purchased a gasoline cook-stove, a machine for vacuum packing meat in freezer bags and a large plastic cooler to be filled with the meat we anticipated bringing back to Seattle.

Both Reuben and myself had a good deal of experience living in tents in east-central Alaska, where arctic conditions prevail, as well as in glacier country north of Haines and the rain forest of southeast Alaska. Reuben had also spent a month in the barren, windswept Aleutian Islands, a place I was content to have missed. At any rate, we knew what to expect a hundred miles north of the Arctic Circle in mid-September.

That night we checked off items on our extensive equipment lists and filled out the five pages of paperwork dealing with our hunting rifles required by Canadian customs. My rifle was a well-used Savage model 99 lever-action in .308 Winchester caliber mounted with a 1.5-5X scope. Reuben was shooting a new bolt action, Savage Model 11 Trophy Hunter XP mounted with a 3-9X scope, in caliber 7mm-08 Remington. These details were evidently of vital interest to Canadian customs officials. We had purchased our caribou tags from Alaska Fish and Game on line a month earlier. Reuben, being more optimistic than I, and had bought two.

We were up early the next morning and began packing our gear into the 2008 Toyota Forerunner belonging to Kim. After, perhaps, five iterations we finally had all the items in the car more or less in the order that we would need them with passports and customs papers up front with us. Reuben had rented a car for his wife's use during our absence; this turned out to be a good thing because her vehicle did not come back in the same condition it left in. At the last moment, Kim presented us with a case of bottled water, a jar of instant coffee, two thousand Canadian dollars and gave Reuben a kiss. It was plain to see she had doubts about this venture.

After about an hour of dense traffic, we turned off the interstate and were soon waiting our turn to cross the border into British Columbia at the Sumas, Washington; we filed the paperwork dealing with our rifles, paid the requisite $25 fee each, and picked up some useful maps of BC and Yukon Territory.

Now, at last, we were on our way to the land of the midnight sun following BC Highway 5 north and turning onto BC Highway 97 at Kamloops. We would follow this road the length of British Columbia to Watson Lake in Yukon Territory.

Ones does not go north, much beyond Kamloops, before farmlands and dairies give way to magnificent mountains exhibiting classic alpine-type glacial features and vastly diminished human populations. Our eyes were straining to see animal life and it was not long before we pulled off the road to photograph herds of elk and bison. Farther north we spotted a mother black bear with two cubs and then two woodland caribou crossing the road in front of us. Dense forests of black spruce and occasional meadows of quaking aspen filled the valleys but declined perceptibly to narrow ribbons along the drainages at higher elevations. Colorful clumps of fireweed lined the disturbed soils adjacent to the highways and presented a striking contrast to the barren, mountainous, glacial vista beyond.

That day, we made it to Prince George, the most populous city in British Columbia at 72,000 souls, and a fine city it appeared to be, proudly proclaiming its origin as an English fur trading post in 1807. Lying at the confluence of the north-flowing Fraser River and the east-flowing Nechako River, Prince George is situated at the geometric center of British Columbia at a driving distance of 558 miles from Seattle. It was a long and tiring day by the time the old geologists carried their heavy duffle bags and rifle cases up to a second story motel room.

We were up bright and early the next morning, had breakfast, gassed the Toyota, and were heading north by 7 a.m. Our route took us due north through mountainous country nearly devoid of human activities except for occasional road maintenance crews. We travelled north for about 150 miles and then swung east, crossing the continental divide at Pine Pass, and were in Dawson Creek for lunch. Along this leg, we saw mountain goats on distant rocky hillsides and three species of wild sheep along the road. By day's end, we were in Ft. Nelson, east of the Northern Rocky Mountains, 502 miles beyond Prince George. The high point of the day came just as we entered the southern outskirts of the village, an excellent view of a beautiful arctic lynx with its large ear tufts, long legs and oversized paws for snow travel.

Ft. Nelson has little to recommend it with a population of only about 4,500 persons and the coldest winter temperatures in British Colombia. At 58°49' north latitude, it should surprise no one that its history began as a fur-trading post of the Northwest Trading Company in 1805. But, there is one surprising fact about this outpost of frigidity. It was the beginning point of the Alaska Highway Project in 1942 when Canada and the US felt the threat of a Japanese invasion via the Aleutian Islands. We were at "Mile Zero" as they like to say in Ft. Nelson.

After breakfast, we drove west traversing across the Northern Rockies again, following the old Alaska Highway, now called Highway 1. We snaked across the border between British Columbia and Yukon Territory five times on our journey to Whitehorse, a distance of 591 miles.

Upon reaching the village of Teslin, we caught our first sight of the almost endless Teslin Lake, a narrow, elongate body of water stretching northwesterly from northern British Colombia to Johnsons Crossing, Yukon Territory, a distance of 75 miles. It was amazing to think that chinook salmon travel the entire length of the mighty Yukon River from the Bering Sea to spawn in this beautiful lake.

As we closed on Whitehorse, we naturally noticed a dramatic increase in human activity and evidence of its year-round population of about 30,000 souls. Whitehorse is not only the capital and largest city in Yukon Territory, it is the only city. I knew from reading Jack London that this city was the southern terminus of the famed Yukon Trail, a 18-inch-wide line of life and death to Dawson City, 334 miles due north.

This set me to thinking about the colorful times of the Klondike gold rush, sparked by the discovery of gold on August 16, 1896. This was followed by a stampede of tens of thousands of would-be miners who endured the terrible hardships of winter dog-sledding over the snow and ice of the Yukon Trail. As we entered the city, I wistfully hoped we might see sourdough prospectors, dancehall girls, and fierce Tlingit warriors but, alas, we were more than a century late. We did find a decent motel and restaurant and went to bed at a reasonable hour.

The next morning, we had a hearty breakfast of pancakes and a slice of delicious rhubarb pie, threw our gear in the Toyota and headed northwest on Highway 1. As we left Whitehorse in the rearview mirror, we passed close to the southern tip of Lake Laberge, rendered immortal by Robert Service in *The Cremation of Sam Magee*. Since, by law, anyone spending much time in Alaska is required to memorize this poem, it struck me that the Klondike poet was obliged to modify the lake's name to "Labarge" to achieve rhyme with the word "marge".

It was moose season in Yukon Territory and Alaska and we saw hunters' vehicles parked along the road, near marshy areas, as well as at nearly every bridge over running water. We saw several moose cows from the car, grazing placidly in ponds but, naturally, no bulls which are the only legal game. Clearly, moose meat is highly regarded by the people living in this rugged region.

We had hoped to make the 590-mile journey to Fairbanks by evening but there were delays caused by road construction projects which, at these latitudes, necessarily must be completed before the end of September. After two such delays, we finally reached Beaver Creek, virtually on the eastern border of Alaska, for lunch at Buckshot Betty's restaurant. It is a colorful place with a hunting-lodge atmosphere and plenty of souvenirs celebrating the gold rush days. Among the guests were two carloads of German-speaking tourists whom we would meet again at the Arctic Circle. We spent this night in Tok, Alaska, some 200 miles southeast of Fairbanks.

The next morning, we were in Fairbanks by 11 a.m. I had not seen the city since 1983 and it was unrecognizable. It is now a bustling major city, not the gold rush relic of my memory. I managed to get the address of the place where Reuben had reserved our satellite telephone into the GPS system of the Toyota and we followed instructions to a small surveyor's shop in a part of the city that did not exist on my last visit. This phone was a requirement by our chartered air service, Brooks Range Aviation, and would be our only method of communication with them for our pickup or in case of emergency.

While Reuben received instructions for operating the unit, I perused the specialized articles used by modern surveyors which cluttered the shelves and walls. I was amazed by the changes in equipment since I had taken a course in subject back in the early sixties.

Returning to the car, I programmed the GPS to take us to the nearest Walmart, evidently, there was more than one in this modern city of Fairbanks. Both Reuben and I had been so obsessed with our personal equipment lists that we completely forgot that we needed numerous items for the camp. We loaded up with a camp cook set, a two-gallon collapsible water jug, a small hatchet, as well as salt and borax for the hides we hoped to bring back. More importantly, we picked up two gallons of fuel for our cook stove and made certain we could buy dry ice for our meat on our return trip.

The Toyota was gassed and crammed to capacity as we followed the Elliott Highway, AK 2, north on the last leg of our journey by car. At mile 78, about five miles southwest of Livengood, we turned north onto Dalton Highway, also known as AK 11, the Pipeline Road and the Haul Road. At least for the first hour, or so, the road was paved and of high quality but we noticed the increase in heavy truck traffic. This road is the only route of supply to the oil industry on the North Slope and the few small communities north of Fairbanks. It more or less parallels the famed Alaska pipeline which can be closely approached at several places. It is impressive.

At mile 57, we crossed the bridge spanning the mighty Yukon River and stopped to take pictures. Reuben, who had driven this route twice before, smiled at my touristic enthusiasm, but the truth was that I had seen this river, just as wide and pristine, quite a number of times from its banks at Circle, Alaska some 160 miles southeast of this bridge. As we expressed rapture over the scenic wonders of the crossing, the two rental cars of the German tourists seen at Buckshot Betty's diner the day before, zoomed by in a rush for the Arctic Circle, which lay some 50 miles north yet. For those who do not know, the Arctic Circle is southernmost latitude where sun can remain continuously above or below horizon for 24 hours.

Resuming our journey, I followed our changes in latitude closely on the compass app of my I-phone as we counted the changes up to 66.5625 degrees north. There was no need for this, of course, as the position is well marked on Dalton Highway by signs, a small parking lot, picnic tables and out houses courteously provided by the National Park Service. We stopped to photograph each other in front of the sign marking the Arctic Circle, but only after courteously waiting for the Germans to photograph each other individually and collectively. With the requisite photos taken, the Germans mounted up and headed south in their cars at high speed. Perhaps they planned to dine again with Buckshot Betty.

As we continued north, the formerly dense thickets of black spruce thinned noticeably and were confined to the lower elevations except for a few straggling and stunted warriors which managed to cling to life along the steep drainages.

It was about 4 p.m. on September 6th when we pulled into the forlorn settlement of Coldfoot, seventy miles north of the circle. Little more than truck stop, it offered gas, a dirty cramped bunkhouse, and a small restaurant filled with souvenirs and T-shirts. We bought gas and paid for a room for two in the bunk house and toted in our rifles and duffle bags in. At the entrance, we were amused by a sign advising us to close the front door to discourage black bears from entering and disturbing the guests. You don't see that every day.

Before dinner, we repacked our gear, donned knee-high rubber boots, long underwear, heavy hunting shirts, and wool caps; everything that would go with us on the hunt was crammed into our weather-proof bags. Our traveling gear, city clothes and shoes would remain with the car. We had a decent and leisurely meal served buffet style and I purchased two T-shirts for my grandchildren featuring a giant naked foot and the words "Coldfoot, Alaska" boldly printed below.

One may ask, what attracts tourists to this forlorn place? We certainly did, but that night, around midnight, we found out. They flock to Coldfoot in September for the auroras, those diffuse, roiling clouds of pink and green in the night time sky that cause tourists to swoon. Their "ooh's" and "ah's" kept us awake till a late hour.

Early the next morning, we used our satellite phone for the first time to call for pick up by Brooks Range Aviation, located in Bettles, Alaska. Bettles is a tiny, but busy settlement, 36 air miles southwest of Coldfoot and not accessible from Dalton Highway except by snow mobile in the winter. We were instructed to have our gear piled on the edge of the airstrip at Pump Station No. 5, about 30 miles south of Coldfoot, by 10 a.m.

It was a bit of a novelty to be driving in a southerly direction but it did not last long and we were soon piling our gear on the logs marking the boundary between the parking lot and the air field. It was sunny and clear, but cold, thanks to a strong northerly breeze. There were, perhaps, 40 cars and trucks in the rough parking lot, all hunters either in their camps or, like us, outward bound. Some very kind moose hunters waiting for their plane offered us steaming cups of coffee which we accepted with sincere gratitude.

The drone of a Cessna 185 engine roused us from our shivering reveries, so we thanked our hosts, and watched the plane taxi toward us with growing excitement. The pilot, Frank, directed the loading of our gear according to size, weight and shape and we were soon in the air heading for Bettles, a settlement with a hotel, a restaurant and, perhaps, 13 year-round residents. But it was also the summer home of three commercial flying services, their employees, rangers for the National Park Service and transient hunters like ourselves. As we circled over the mile-long gravel runway, we could see two clusters of float planes tied up at loading docks on the Koyukuk River as well as large hangars and fueling facilities. We quickly realized that this remote place, at 66° 55' north latitude, was an important air traffic hub between Fairbanks and the North Slope oil fields.

When the Cessna cut its engine, a pickup truck appeared immediately and two young men loaded it up with our gear and hauled it to the hangar entrance. Reuben and I pulled out those items that were to remain in Bettles including our meat-bagging machine, ice cooler, the hard cases for the rifles and a few other minor items and deposited them on a tarp inside the spacious hangar. The remaining equipment destined to go to the field with us was then weighed and transported to the loading docks for the float planes.

While we were in the hangar we took a short tour, examining the tarps of hunters who had recently returned. The dozens of moose and caribou antlers were impressive and even a little intimidating for the two old geologists who had yet to prove themselves. Several successful hunters told us their stories as they cut and bagged their meat. One guy claimed that he had shot his caribou bull at *640 measured yards*. We laughed about that one.

We went to the offices of Brooks Range Aviation to deal with paperwork related to our hunt, pay our fees and to determine just where we were going to hunt for the next week or so. The pilots and returning hunters play an important role in the selection of hunting sites for caribou as they see where herds gather and can guess which passes they are likely to use in their migration from the North Slope where they graze throughout the summer.

Summer's end is the signal for these vast herds to begin their 2,000-to-3,000-kilometer southward trek for breeding and calving in the needleleaf forest lands, or taiga, of the Porcupine River in west-central Yukon Territory. It is the longest migration of any land mammal.

The hunting strategy is simple enough, select a lake suitable for float-planes, south of the passes in the northern Brooks Range that lead down into the Noatak Valley. After some discussion, including one with a pilot in the air above the Brooks Range, a small nameless lake, just beyond the western border of the Gates of the Arctic National Park, was chosen as our destination. An hour later, our De Havilland Beaver, a four-seated, single engine, high-wing craft, equipped with pontoon floats was loaded and we were again in the air heading northwest to our lake, 125 miles away.

We followed the valley of the east-flowing Alatna River and marveled at the spectacular mountain glaciers and large-scale folds in the rocks below. Reuben, sitting in front, chatted with the pilot but I could not follow their conversation from a back seat over the hum of the powerful engine. I was content to photograph the spectacular geological features sliding by my window.

After about an hour of flight time, we crossed a drainage divide and followed the west-flowing Noatak River and our lake was soon visible. It was a sausage-shaped body, eight miles long and one mile wide, elongate in the north-south direction, but looked very small from our seats in the Beaver. A few lonely black spruce and quaking aspen could be seen in the alluvium along course of the Noatak River but died out immediately in the permafrost terrain at the northern edge of the valley.

"Tundra" is the word for the land we were entering. A treeless land of permafrost where cold winds and 60-day growing seasons limited vegetation to dwarfish, shallow-rooted, clumping tussock grasses, mosses, liverworts, cotton grass, cushion plant, arctic poppy, arctic willow and, most importantly, lichens, the main food of Barren Land caribou. This was a land that was marshy and wet in summer from snow melt that could not drain though frozen soil. A land where sloping soil layers were deformed into curious, rumpled lobes extending from the steep valley walls, a few miles north of our lake, nearly to the banks of the Noatak River. This creeping soil action, called "solifluction", is the dominant form of erosion at extreme latitudes where the all too brief summer heat melts only the upper few inches of frozen soil on south-facing slopes.

It was not an unlovable landscape, but it was an inherently dangerous one because of its lack of fuel and open exposure to the elements. One had to respect this, particularly in September which is a month that will bring not only the autumnal equinox, but also icing of the lakes and the first snows of winter.

Our pilot glided at low altitude over the entire length of the lake checking for objects in the water and gaging the intensity of the wave action at the north end where, ultimately, he would land us. The plane banked sharply to the east and set down into the wind about a mile from shore and taxied to a rocky point on the northernmost shore.

The three of us formed a line to unload our equipment, the pilot standing on the pontoon, Reuben knee deep in the cold water and me on the rocks. We had weighed our gear at Bettles and were slightly below the 800-pound limit imposed by the flying service. Now, it all had to carried up a steep, south-facing, muddy gulley to the nearest flat place that would serve as our home for an unknown number of days. As we contemplated this task, our pilot, Frank, shook our hands, wished us luck and clambered back into the Beaver. In less than a minute he was airborne and heading toward Bettles, our nearest, and only point of contact with the outside world.

As we watched the plane shrink to a flyspeck, I was reflecting that, here I was, at the northernmost geographical point in my 50 year career, nearly 68 degrees, and it was the afternoon of the 7th of September with a stiff, cold wind coming out of the south over a cold, nameless lake. A couple of old men could wind up in trouble in a situation like this. We each grabbed an armload of gear and trucked the 10 slippery yards up the slope to our new home. One trip sufficed to show us an abundance of tracks left by grizzlies and wolves, not unexpected, of course, but still something to think about. I loaded my rifle and leaned it against a shrubby, stunted willow decorated with tangled streamers of dried caribou velvet. We were in the right place, evidently, both for caribou and other denizens of the arctic.

It took about ten trips up the now slimy access gulley by both of us to get the gear into an untidy pile. We unfolded our camp chairs, and sat down to rest with our backs to the wind and facing an unwarming sun which was low in the west. "What do you think?" Reuben queried me.

"I think this is a shitty place to camp, too much exposure to this damned wind, and way too many griz tracks" I answered "but we have too much gear to do anything else and, since we will have to carry our water up from the lake, this will have to do".

"Yeah, I agree. It is a bad place, alright, but I can't see anything better close by. Why, did we bring so much gear?" Reuben asked. "Besides, if we get two caribou bulls we will have as much as a thousand pounds more to deal with".

"We could encourage the bears to eat it, so we wouldn't have to carry it" I volunteered.

"That's an idea, but it would get us in trouble with the fish-and-game guys who will probably be on hand to check us out when we get back to Bettles. Besides, I have to bring back meat to keep my wife happy so I can keep going on hunts" replied Reuben with a grin. "Ok, the first thing is to get the tent set up. It is still in the box I bought it in".

It was a very high quality tent, meaning it was complicated to set up, but after two abortive attempts, we managed. We needed our small axe to drive the metal stakes into the hard ground but when the job was finished we had a secure, windproof structure that provided a sleeping room and a separate small outer room to keep clothes, boots, and rifles out of the elements. We threw our mummy bags and air mattresses into the tent and retreated to our camp chairs to admire our work.

"That is one hell of a tent you have there, Reuben. Must have set you back 500 bucks or more".

"Yeah, it was closer to a thousand, but I knew we would need something really good this far north and I will be able to use it again when I deer hunt in Colorado in late October. Let's get the stove out and make some coffee".

I scrambled and slid my way down to the lake and filled our collapsible, two-gallon jug with water while he pried the stove out of its packaging, filled the tank with Coleman fuel, pumped up the tank pressure and managed to light it in spite of the wind. Even with the protective wind guards of the stove in place, the wind managed to blow the flames sideways, away from the coffee pot, making the effort difficult and inefficient. Finally, we sat hunching and shivering against the wind, collars up and wool sock caps pulled low and cradling our coffee cups as if they were precious gems.

"Christ, this is good coffee" I chattered out. "We are going to have to rig a wind screen in front of the stove so we can use our fuel more efficiently".

"Yep, I was thinking the same thing. We can use that 8-by-10 plastic tarp and the rods we brought for the meat tent, but driving them into this ground will be a job".

"It will, but we can't waste the two gallons of fuel we brought. If we run out in this country before we get our bulls, it won't be a joke. I can see there won't be any gathering buffalo chips to build campfires" I volunteered, taking a big slurp of coffee.

We chatted idly as we finished off the coffee and I began thinking about what we might have to contend with if the weather took a turn for the worse. At this latitude, we could expect nearly 14 hours of daylight in early September but this would decrease systematically by about six minutes per day with the approaching equinox on September 22. Night temperatures in mid-summer would have been in the upper 30's, but now they would be in the upper 20's in transition to winter temperatures which would be below zero in another month or two. Of course, there would be snow at some point and our lake would certainly freeze. I could see patches of snow in shaded clefts in the major mountains jutting up two or three miles north of us but that was snow that fell last winter, not new snow.   My experience in the Circle region had taught me that snow fell in every calendar month, so obviously, we could anticipate that we would see it here, if we stayed late enough in September.

The sun was now shining brightly, the wind had backed off, and we were feeling pretty good about our situation.   Our camp had been brought into passable order, except for the wind screen, which could wait for tomorrow.   Our rifles were loaded and standing ready at arms-length from our chairs. We could not hunt on this day because of the strictly enforced state law forbidding hunting on any day that one is in the air. But we could fish, and there was a lake in front of us and we supposed it to be teeming with voracious arctic charr, a very sporting fish of the trout family.

An hour of fruitless casting and the loss of several lures convinced us both of our error.   However, during the fishing, Reuben saw a lone wolf streaking east along the edge of the lake. Our first animal sighting!   We entertained ourselves by constructing a number of ribald scenarios to explain why this wolf had been abandoned by his pack, but these add nothing to the present story.

We sat facing a prominent pass through the mountains north of us from which our caribou would come. Their arrival would be, almost certainly, heralded by a cloud of dust if the herd had any size. The hundreds of caribou tracks between our camp and the lake shore assured us that we were on a major migration route as did the eerie streamers of antler velvet dangling from every bush of any size.

We considered the possibility of simply waiting in our chairs, with cups of coffee, for the herd to show up and shoot them on the spot. There had been joking about "tent-flap caribou" often during the months leading up to this day and we could now see that this was an actual possibility. However, the grizzly tracks that also ringed our camp suggested that this might not be a good idea. Gutting two 500 pound animals in camp might have unpleasant consequences, so, we resolved on no hunting from the camp site.

Dinner was the next topic of conversation and I ticked off the menu selections from the 20 packets of dehydrated meals that I had carried from Texas. All that was required was two cups of boiling water poured into the foil pouches and stir. I had tried one of the meals at home before I flew to Seattle and found it to be passable, but very bland. To counter this, I also brought a sandwich bag containing about a cup of ground pequin peppers which are 20-40 times hotter than jalapenos. There would be no bland meals.

We selected "Santa Fe Fiesta" as our first entree and set a pot of lake water on the Coleman to boil. It is amazing how the hissing sound of a gas stove and its small bluish flame can hypnotize two men, even men with Ph.D. degrees, like ourselves. I imagined that we both were thinking of the famous Jack London story, "To Build a Fire", I know I was. Without the wind, our water was soon boiling and I poured the contents of the pouch into the pot, stirred, and added a couple of pinches of salt and pequin powder and dinner was served. It turned out to be a *chili-con-carne* thing with beef, corn, black beans and some other vegetable material that I could not identify. It was not a five-star meal, of course, but it was not bad, considering that we were at 68° north, in tundra country and had no arctic charr. While we had the stove on, we heated water for the cleanup and made tea which we drank as we contemplated the sun sinking in the west and the magnificent wild country surrounding us.

The sun was just setting and Reuben was itching to have a look at the area surrounding our camp and took off with his rifle and a small pack of survival gear. I got out a large map of the state of Alaska and tried to locate our approximate position on it. I was able to find our lake, even though it was the size of an ant on this map. The lake was situated about 12 miles north of Noatak River, something like 20 miles east of Lake Matcharak, and about 25 miles south of Midas Creek. These were the only named geographical features the map offered in our vicinity and they were not particularly close or comforting to isolated men on foot. According to the map, we were now some 88 miles north of the circle, at a latitude of about 67.8 degrees.

As darkness began to fall, Reuben tramped into camp. He had seen no animals but did report seeing muskox dung and tracks in addition to ubiquitous bear and caribou sign. It was growing noticeably colder without the sun rays, so we decided to make more tea and munch a few breakfast bars as a post-fiesta dessert.

We discussed the local geology as revealed by the pebbles lying around the camp. They were all low-grade metamorphic rocks derived from the mountains north of us, slates, phyllites and green schists, which are common enough in Alaskan mountain terrains and not of much interest to either of us. We lamented the lack of wood for a campfire and were forced to go to bed earlier than we wished to get warm. This had to be accomplished one man at a time so that each had room to unroll his mummy bag, inflate his mattress, get out of our heavy clothes and wriggle into the bag. In my case, because my sleeping bag was an old one, I inserted a newly-purchased bag liner which claimed to give 10-15 additional degrees of protection. We were eager for morning and the beginning of our bucket-list hunt.

The next morning broke sunny, but cold, thanks to a strong south wind off the lake. We managed two cups of coffee and a breakfast bar each and took off in different directions with rifles loaded and day packs shouldered. I headed in a northwesterly direction for about a half mile and found a small knoll where I could sit with my outline broken by stunted willows and observe the mountain pass north of me. The topography in this area was marked by low rocky hills and swales with superposed hummocks and depressions produced by solifluction movement. In front of me, there were foothills which systematically grew higher as they approached the true mountains of the mighty Brooks Range. In spite of the cold wind, I managed to sit quietly, looking for signs of life, for about two hours before I was forced to start walking to get warm. I munched another breakfast bar, more out of boredom than hunger, until I finally saw movement about two hundred yards away on my left. I threw my scope up on what turned out to be some kind of a weasel-like rodent. I studied the poor thing for an hour as it worked around a pile of rocks in a search for food.

Next, my attention fell on a peculiar white object located at the mouth of the pass, some two miles distant, where I expected caribou to appear at any moment. I studied this odd feature through my rifle scope for a good 15 minutes before I concluded it was an angular boulder of milky quartz, five or six feet in diameter. That meant there were quartz veins cutting the metamorphic rocks exposed in the pass, but this contributed nothing to the business at hand. About noon, the wind died down and I returned to my knoll where I sat in boredom until about 3 o'clock. I focused on the plants around me and tried to estimate the number of species growing within 10 feet of my position. I lost count at 45. I saw no more animals, not even a bird overhead, so I returned my attention to the quartz boulder but it had not changed its position. I went back to our camp in a deflated mood.

I found Reuben busily cooking eggs and bacon from a pouch for our belated breakfast and he had made coffee. His game report was not quite as dismal as mine, he had seen an eagle in the distance and eagle trumps weasel. We had a lazy meal and discussed rigging the tarp for a windbreak, but since there was no wind at the moment, this task was postponed to the morrow.

I grabbed my fishing rod and went down to the lake determined to catch one of those elusive charr. I was unsuccessful, but did manage to get water in both of my rubber knee boots. We spent what remained of the day discussing geological topics and keeping our eyes on the pass for a dust cloud. There was no dust and we went to the mummy bags early to escape the cold.

The next morning, we were up early. The sun was shining brightly but gave no warmth and we had to endure a very cold wind off the lake. The stove was difficult to light and we struggled to make coffee and huddled over our cups when we finally succeeded. We discussed breakfast options and elected oatmeal but someone needed to fetch water from the lake. Rock-paper-scissors decided the issue, and I went with our plastic jug down to the shore and waded out not quite to my boot tops and filled the container. I could not miss noticing that a tiny fringe of ice had formed at the water's edge.

The oatmeal was boiling away and we were anticipating a warm meal when Reuben shouted "Dust!" I looked toward the pass and, sure enough, there was an obvious cloud and, below it, I could see the gleaming antlers of the leaders, still at least a mile away. They were coming directly toward us at a systematic, distance-eating trot. Breakfast was forgotten, the stove was shut down, and we grabbed our rifles and ran to a clump of bushes some fifty yards north of camp and waited breathlessly. Our gloves were off, we checked our rifles to make sure we had live rounds in the chambers and waited. The herd disappeared behind a low hill but we expected them to reappear any second and fought to maintain our composure. This was the moment!

But, the moments of waiting stretched into minutes. We looked at each other, silently asking "Where the hell are they?" Another minute or two passed but we saw no sign of the herd. "Let's move up on them" I whispered to Reuben. He nodded, and we rose from our kneeling positions and carefully crept forward to a low, grassy ridge that blocked our view. I crawled the last few feet toward the ridge top on my hands and knees and, even before I had a view of the horse-shoe-shaped depression beyond, I could see, what appeared in my excited state, to be a forest of antlers in gentle swaying motion.

I wriggled forward until I could see into the depression; 50 or 60 caribou bulls were lying in the tundra grasses, sheltering from the chilling wind! There was not a single cow among them. I backed down a few feet from the brow of the ridge and looked at Reuben, he had seen them as well and motioned to me that he was going to take a position on the west side of the north-opening horse shoe. I gave him 30 seconds and then, very carefully, crawled back on my stomach to the ridge top with my rifle in front of me and began surveying the herd for a good bull. The closest bulls were a mere 30 yards from my position but they were in a very tight group and I feared my round would hit a second animal. I looked the entire group over carefully, there was no indication that they were aware of the presence of humans, so I took my time. There was one bull, a big one with magnificent antlers, with no other animals behind him. He was about 60 yards distant, facing my direction, and lying at about a 45-degree angle to my line of fire. So, I carefully put my rifle in position, zeroed in on the base of his neck, took a deep breath, let half of it out, and squeezed off a round.

I don't know what I expected, but before the sound of my shot dissipated, I was looking at an empty depression, absolutely empty. The dull, sinking feeling of failure instantly began spreading from the pit of my stomach, but then a shot rang out. A low ridge shielded this action and the fleeing herd from me, but I got to my feet as rapidly as I could, my hands shaking, and climbed the obstructing hillock to find a smiling Reuben and two caribou bulls on the ground about five yards apart. One killed by each of us. We shook hands, embraced and, perhaps, danced around a bit. And why not? We were two septuagenarians who had just scratched off a major item on our bucket-list well above the Arctic Circle.

Reuben had his camera on his belt so we inspected our respective kills, complimented each other on the size of the antlers, and took the requisite posed photos trying to look as serious as Ernest Hemingway after shooting a man-eating leopard in Kenya. Of course, caribou are not man eaters, they devour lichen, but no matter, we were as happy as two old hunters could be.

After pictures and mutual congratulations, the first order of business was to field dress the animals, a subject that no one wants described. However, there is much of interest in the food, dentition and digestive system of caribou. First, there is the food itself, which I have described as "lichen", that grows prolifically on rocks and in the thin, poor soils of tundra country. The favored lichen is commonly called "caribou moss"; it is a low-growing, pale green to grey, spongy-looking material with an extremely branching habit. It grows very slowly but is well adapted to arctic climates and abundant. Lichen, although quite indigestible by humans, provides the caribou with carbohydrates for heat and vitamins for nourishment.

This simple-looking "moss" is actually a combination of both algae and fungi which live together in complex symbiosis. Since upper incisors are lacking in caribou, the moss is ripped off with the lower incisors pressing the plant material against the leathery roof of the mouth and is swallowed without chewing. This is an adaptation that allows ruminants to quickly gather large quantities of food and retire to safety from predators, mainly wolves, for later digestion. The initial digestive stage is the rumen where the lichen is attacked by bacteria and regurgitated later in safety. The caribou chews this in the fashion of cows as "cud" using the upper and lower grinding teeth and then swallow it again. The animal is generally in a relaxed prone position during this process and the jaws can be seen vigorously working. In the second stage, the masticated cud bypasses the rumen and is delivered to the reticulum and, from there, to the omasum. The function of these two stages is to squeeze excess water out of the digesting product. Finally, the fourth chamber, the abomasum, passes the nutrients into the bloodstream. These are the so-called "four stomachs of ruminants". It is a complex process, isn't it? I only wished I had known something of it when I was handling these organs.

We returned to camp, both to finish our interrupted breakfast, and pick up the tools needed to butcher and bag our meat. We re-heated our oatmeal, drank two cups of coffee each, grabbed my rifle, our skinning and meat knives, our 8 x10 foot plastic tarp and Reuben's new Wyoming saw. The latter was a collapsible affair with several blades made for cutting bone and a very handy tool for the job before us. We took up a package of 10 large white muslin "caribou bags" to put the meat in and a special "meat-hauling" back pack for transporting the meat back to camp.

We were in camp less than an hour but when we returned to the kill site, a beautiful red arctic fox was already feeding on the offal. He scampered away at our approach but kept a close eye on the proceedings, no doubt planning to return after we left. He had a long wait.

We started the process at about 11 a.m. by jointly skinning Reuben's bull and it was no easy matter to remove the hide of a 500-600-pound animal on the ground. It required both men to roll the animal over to complete the process. I removed the rear haunches, which weighed about 80 pounds each, and placed them on our tarp. It took both of us to put the larger pieces in the bags. Lucky Reuben put on the transport pack, we adjusted the straps, and loaded him up with one haunch which was all he could handle. He staggered toward camp while I quartered and bagged the rest of his caribou. He returned, just as I finished with his bull and started skinning my own; I loaded him up with another 80 pounds of meat and he dutifully repeated the trip.

It was 9 p.m. and very nearly dark when the last of the meat went on Reuben's back. We were totally exhausted and limped back to camp with me carrying the rifle, butchering gear and bloody tarp. My back was killing me from stooping all day.

We left the hides and antlers where they were to deal with on the following day. I knew that Reuben had purchased a second caribou tag, so during this final trek, I informed him that, if he tried to fill this tag, I would have to shoot him and let the fox and his brethren eat his carcass. He was in total agreement.

We had done a good day's work, considering our age, and there were eight large muslin bags of fresh meat, perhaps 500 or 600 pounds, lined up along the lake shore. I wanted to go directly to bed, but my buddy insisted that we wash up and have a bowl of soup before seeking the warmth of our mummy bags. The temperature felt like it could be in the low twenties and a north wind was mounting, although in our weary state, we did not notice this ominous change.

The next morning, I rose around 7 a.m. in response to nature's call. It was very cold and I had trouble getting into my frozen clothes. A thin sheet of ice had formed on the inside roof of the tent from our condensing breath. When, at last, my personal business was discharged, I faced toward the east to greet the sun and was astounded to see three suns on the horizon.

Three suns, think of it! I knew what it meant from reading Jack London's Klondike tales but, in spite of all my time in tundra country, I had never seen it. But, of course, I had never been in the arctic this late in September. It was the famous "sundog effect" generated by refraction of solar rays through clouds of platy, hexagonal ice crystals which, in other circumstances, would have drawn not only admiration, but a discussion of the optics behind the phenomena. Now, it was an ominous threat of the arrival of very cold air from the north.

My gasp of surprise must have awakened Reuben who was soon at my side. We were dazzled by the sight of the two spikey sundogs, or mock suns, symmetrically disposed along a circular halo around of the true sun. Each "dog" displayed classic dispersion from red-orange on the bulbous, solar edge to blue-green on the tapered edge away from the sun. No offense to Jack, but it was an awesome sight, so much more stirring than his descriptions. Wordlessly, we ran for our cameras.

We knew by the sundogs that we were in for bad weather and even before we could get the Coleman fired up we were immersed in a fog of fine-granular ice crystals that peppered exposed skin like thousands of hypodermic needles. The low foothills north of us were rapidly turning white. It was almost like being in a dust storm but, of course, much colder. While our coffee water was heating, I began the much-delayed erection of our wind shelter while Reuben went to the lake for water. I lashed the aluminum poles for our meat tent into three tripods and secured the bloody tarp to a line running along the tripods and staked it at both ends. The result was a fairly secure, v-shaped wall about five feet high with its apex facing into the vicious north wind. It shielded our small folding table and stove admirably.

When Reuben returned with the water, he reported that ice was forming along the edges of the lake. It was not good news. We drank our coffee huddled as much as possible in the lee of our new shelter.

Our first item of business was to retrieve our antlers and hides, so we loaded our salt bag and box of 20-mule-team borax onto Reuben's meat pack, I grabbed a few odd pieces of rope and my rifle and we headed out into the teeth of a gritty, cold north wind.

The mountains north of us had disappeared in the white that was invading our small, bleak world. Yesterday's trek now seemed like a spring-time stroll in the park. When we arrived at the kill site, our friend the red fox was there to greet us and he was joined by a great golden eagle. Both departed as soon as we came into view but the eagle had some difficulty flying in the stiff wind. I wondered where the nearest tree could be for this magnificent bird to perch in.

I spread a generous coating of salt and borax on each hide, then rolled and tied each into a bundle. Reuben nested one set of antlers into the other, lashed them together into one very awkward and heavy entity and, together, we managed to secure them to the pack frame. I slung the hides over my shoulders, grabbed my rifle and we set off for camp. Visibility was declining rapidly but the trail Reuben had created yesterday was easy to follow and, with the wind at our back, we almost sailed into camp.

We sat in camp drinking hot tea and assessed our situation. We had used up nearly a gallon of Coleman fuel and had only one gallon in reserve. We had plenty of meat, naturally. True, it was now frozen, but we had no cooking oil which we would need if we didn't want to gnaw it raw. If Brooks Range Aviation could not pick us up today or tomorrow, we might have to be resupplied. If the lake froze over completely, and that now looked possible, they would not be able to put a float plane down to get us out. Reuben got the satellite telephone out, and made the call.

They could not pick us up today, maybe tomorrow, but no promises. Other groups had priority and their lakes were beginning to ice up as well. "Don't panic, we won't forget you" was the reassuring advice they gave us. "Call again tomorrow at the same time".

The icy snow had let up and we could see the sun, only one of them now, as it was about mid-day, but it was still windy and cold, well below freezing. I was thinking we might not see the temperature above the freezing point before we got back to Bettles, and maybe not even then.

Reuben decided we should eat a caribou steak before the bears or wolves got to it and went down to our meat pile and began cutting away. I yelled down to him to cut off some lard as well as meat so we could fry them in our only skillet. There is not much lard on a caribou carcass but he managed to get enough to fry two steaks, but the small size of our skillet made it necessary to cook them one at a time. Given our situation, however, it seemed like a Viking feast.

We worried about our meat and how to keep it out of the jaws of predators and how to cut it up once it became hard frozen. I suggested we put a haunch in Reuben's sleeping bag but he would not entertain this idea. We then decided to leave it where it was, at a distance of about 25 yards from our tent, and use the Wyoming saw to cut it.

Fuel was the problem that threatened us the most, without it we could not make use of our dehydrated meals or melt ice for the water we would need every day. We walked down to the lake and checked the progress of the ice. Slabs about ½ inch thick were forming along the shore, breaking off in the wave action and floating out into the lake.

We spent the remainder of the day worrying about our fuel, even as it was further diminished by making another pot of tea and cooking up ramen noodle soup. We put a heavy coat over our water jug to slow down it's rate of freezing, checked the ice thickness at the shore line hourly, and discussed what to do with our meat cache.

We knew that wolves or bears would be able to scent the meat, as well as ourselves, from as much as a mile away. The scent of humans might be a deterrent, but only if they had learned to fear men. What were the chances that these marauding predators had ever encountered men in this remote place? We considered taking a haunch of caribou back to the butchering site as a sort of sacrifice to the gods of gluttony to buy time but decided they would consider this merely an hors d'oeuvre and feel, understandably, entitled to the full entrée. Besides, we had worked too hard for our meat to give it away without a fight. So, in the end, we decided to guard the meat and tent military style by alternately standing guard through the night, with a rifle and flashlight on our lap, and changing off at two-hour intervals.

I took the first watch at 10 p.m. and Reuben went to the tent. We would both be getting less than a good night's sleep. There was no wind, but it was cold, damned cold. I had my heaviest clothes on, gloves, wool cap pulled low and parka hood snugged up but found I could sit no more than 10 minutes at a time without walking around to keep my feet warm. Rubber boots, even with thick wool socks and in-soles, were not ideal for these conditions.

I patrolled a semicircle around the camp at a distance of about 50 yards, keeping the tent in sight by moon light and checking my watch compulsively. It was a long two hours. I called Reuben at midnight and crawled, gratefully, into my bag. It was heavenly, I assure you. We passed the night without incident, but daylight found us both exhausted and unwilling to climb out of our bags to greet the sun. I am ashamed to admit that it was 10 a.m. before we managed to struggle into frozen clothes and socks and begin our morning routine. We found our water jug frozen solid, so while Reuben fiddled with the stove, I took our largest pot and the small camp axe down to the lake, chopped a hole in the ice, now an inch and a half thick, and returned with water for coffee.

We made breakfast which necessitated opening our second, and last, can of Coleman fuel. Reuben got on the satellite phone and spoke with our people in Bettles. They agreed to airdrop fuel and cooking oil and told us they needed at least eight inches of ice, minimum, before they could pick us up by ski plane. They advised us to relax, enjoy the scenery, two other groups were in the same position, and they had never lost a hunter. We complained that it was cold, damned cold, they laughed and said "This is Alaska, boys".

Two hours later, we heard the drone of an airplane engine and soon the De Havilland Beaver that initially dropped us was circling above, still mounted on floats. We waved at Frank, the pilot, he waggled his wings, and a red parachute attached to a box began slowly drifting down to us. We ran to the box and attacked it with our hunting knives like twin Robinson Crusoe's marooned for years instead of half a day. Supply by parachute seems always to draw this response from the insecure men below. They do not cherish the feeling of loss of control.

In addition to the four gallons of fuel and gallon of cooking oil we requested, they sent us a bag of chocolate-chip cookies, a large box of candy bars, and a big jar of instant coffee. We sawed off a couple of thick frozen caribou steaks and fried them up in a party atmosphere. If we had a bottle of whiskey, it would have been emptied in an hour.

Perhaps we should have asked for whiskey, but we didn't, so it was coffee and steak. Just as we finished our repast, small, feathery snowflakes began to fall and, within an hour, our world was transformed to a scene from Doctor Zhivago.

The thickness of the shoreline ice was now a full two inches and we attempted to calculate how many days it would take to reach eight inches. This proved impossible because we had neglected to note the relationship between time and thickness. We rectified this by scratching 2:35 pm = 2", onto the plastic jug containing our cooking oil and repeating our measurements every two hours. At 6:35 p.m. we had 2.25 inches of ice which meant that the thickness was increasing at a rate of ¼ inch in 4 hours, or 1 inch per 16 hours. So, instead of drinking whiskey, we occupied ourselves in mentally calculating how long it would take to reach the all-important eight-inch thickness. After a number of missteps, we finally arrived at a value of 92 hours or 3.8 days, assuming the rate of thickness increase was constant. We then debated whether the rate of freezing should be considered a constant. Intuitively, it seemed that it would increase as it got colder, so our value of 3.8 days should be taken as the maximum wait for our pick up. This is how science guys think and, rightly or wrongly, it kept our minds occupied with thoughts of physics rather than of bears and wolves.

Reuben said he was tired and asked if I would take the first watch from 10 p.m. to midnight. I agreed and got my flashlight and rifle and took my position in a camp chair. It was cold, of course, we had not seen temperatures above freezing since the day of the kill, and now the feathery snow had changed to ice pellets that stung exposed skin mercilessly. I positioned my chair in the lee of our windbreak and tried to be alert. There were no stars or moonlight but the snow reflected what light there was so I could see our meat cache pretty clearly from where I sat. Every 15 or 20 minutes I made my customary half-circle around the camp, now making loud crunching sounds on the accumulating ice.

I must have dozed off around 11:30, or so, but was awakened by loud crunching and snuffling. I instantly knew it was a bear, even before I saw it, and yelled "Reuben" as loud as I could. I threw my rifle up to my shoulder but, in my excitement, forgot to remove my gloves and could not slide the safety off. I backed up a few paces as the brute, and he was a big one, stared at me with a fierce look in those brown eyes that I took for carnivorous desire. Clearly, he was not here to sell Charmin toilet tissue.

I tore off my gloves and backed up another few paces to set up a shot that would not go into the tent where Reuben was struggling to get out of his bag. Unfortunately, I backed off the embankment and tumbled backwards down the rock-hard slope of frozen mud and actually rolled out onto the lake ice several yards from the shore. I scrambled to my feet only to find that I had lost my rifle in the fall. I could see it hung up in some low brush half-way up the incline.

Evidently, the bear lost interest in me and became preoccupied with slapping the tent which, because of the springy fiberglass support rods, instantly returned to its original shape. After a few moments, he tired of this and pounced upon the tent, flattening it completely, breaking the guy lines and support rods, and tearing out the loops securing it to its stakes in the ground. He rolled one way, then the other, snarling and slashing with all four paws and entangling himself in the tent fabric. It was chaos beyond anything I had ever seen and poor Reuben was at the epicenter.

I should have retrieved my rifle during this violent scene and shot the marauding beast, but I didn't. I slipped and fell hard on the ice and was lying there, paralyzed, while that ferocious bastard mangled my buddy, our tent, and our sleeping bags.

At length, and I don't know if that means seconds or minutes, the bear extricated itself from the remains of our tent and fixed his attention on me. I managed to gain my feet and backed up a few paces on the ice and waited to see what he would do. Retrieving the rifle was not an option now. Now, the sole option appeared to be ascertaining if humans can outrun grizzly bears on ice and I did not like the odds.

He quickly came down the slope, stepping on my rifle during the process and stared at me from the shoreline. He gingerly placed his forepaws on the ice, it held, so he came forward slowly and carefully to the point where the ice was supporting his entire weight. Satisfied that the ice would support him, he lowered his head and came for me at a conservative pace, not a full, high-speed charge. I rapidly backed away from the shore line maintaining eye contact with the slavering monster and fervently prayed to all Saints of Ireland that the ice became thinner away from the shore. For twenty minutes, or so, this deadly minuet continued, me retreating about 10 yards, the bear methodically advancing the same distance.

It was evident that the animal was concerned about breaking through the ice and that was the only reason he did not charge. If he had charged at the shoreline, I would have been a goner, but now, we were something like 60 yards beyond the shore, the ice had to be less than three inches thick, and my confidence was mounting. After all, I was 200 pounds and my ursine stalker must have weighed in at least 1200 pounds.

I backed another 10 yards and actually could feel small

fractures propagating under my boots and prepared myself to sprawl flat on the ice. Evidently, the same thing was happening to the man-eater before me who stopped short, began sniffing the ice surface beneath his paws, and then dropped into a low crouching position. But it was too late, I could hear the ice cracking beneath him. He rapidly pivoted to his right, in an attempt to retreat shoreward, but in doing so, he momentarily lifted his front paws, placing his full weight on his hind legs. It was too much and the ice gave way. Mr. Griz clawed the air, issued a furious yowl of protest and crashed through the surface, creating an impressive geyser of water and ice fragments.

I watched the spot where he disappeared for 15 minutes, unconscious of the cold, constantly anticipating the marrow-chilling scenario of a pissed-off griz blasting up through the ice beneath my feet. But there was no agitation or movement in the water, nothing, only the black silence of a cold arctic night.

Making a wide circuit around the hole, which was already beginning to re-freeze, I made my way back to the camp site with my numbed hands deep in the pockets of my parka. I expected to find Reuben in pieces and that I would have to place his remains in our extra caribou bags, an ugly job, but I could not leave him here to be devoured by wolves.

As I got closer to shoreline, I perceived a moving figure at the camp site which, at first, I took for another bear. It was not a bear, or a wolf for that matter, it was Reuben himself, alive and in one piece. He cheered and clapped as I struggled up the slope. Evidently, I was a hero. He had gathered my rifle, gloves and flashlight and made coffee during my ordeal on the lake and handed me a fresh cup as I settled into a camp chair. "I didn't expect to find you in one piece" I told him.

"Yeah, I figured you were dead meat, too, at first. I suppose you know you left your rifle behind. Not many guys have the stones to face down a griz without a weapon. Pretty cute trick, luring that brute out onto thin ice. As for me, I am a tough old bastard to kill, but that griz did for our tent and bags and scrambled up our gear. We going to be forced to sit up all night" replied Reuben with a wry grin.

I had to ask. "Why the hell didn't you shoot the bear while we were dancing on the ice, instead of making coffee?"

He gave me a serious look and answered "I figured the fall your gun took screwed up the sighting of your scope and I might hit you instead. Besides, I could plainly see you had everything under control". I was not satisfied with this, but let it pass. We congratulated each other in being alive. We knew we were both lucky.

Reuben was sporting a nasty four-inch gash on his forehead and I asked "Is that from a griz claw?"

"Hell, if I know, maybe. All I remember is that my world was as dark as a whore's heart, spinning like a tornado, gear was flying everywhere and a thousand-pound bear was on top of me. I don't know where my rifle and my boots are". He held up his feet which were encased with multiple pairs of socks, the outer ones being mine.

We spent the remainder of the night drinking coffee, eating candy bars and retelling our individual accounts. It was noticeable that in each iteration our actions became more purposeful and the old geologists became more heroic.

When morning light came, it was still snowing lightly. We measured the overnight snow accumulation at four inches and the shore ice thickness at five and a half inches. Then we untwisted and shook out the remains of the tent and mummy bags and began sorting our gear into piles. Reuben was, of course, most anxious to find his boots, I was most anxious to find the satellite telephone.

Virtually all the gear was intact, clothes, food, ammo, Reuben's rifle and boots, even the fishing rods which had been parked against a bush beyond the tent. Except for the loss of the tent, we were still in pretty good shape. The sleeping bags had some rips in the outer nylon shells but we were able to patch these with duct tape so the insulating down remained inside. Our self-inflating mattresses were both ripped and flat but would serve as a floor for our future shelter. Our dehydrated food supply and meat cache were completely intact. So, all in all, we had to admit that our position was reasonably tolerable, considering the exciting events of the preceding night. At least, neither of the old geologists were residing in a caribou bag.

Reuben was pissed about his tent, of course, but we salvaged two large pieces which could be fashioned into a crude lean-to that we could sleep under if it came to that. We also had the tarp presently serving as a windbreak and plenty of rope. We tested the satellite phone. It still worked. Reuben called the air service in Bettles, told them our story and gave them the current ice thickness. "Pick up tomorrow afternoon, weather permitting" they told us, "enjoy the scenery and wildlife". With this unneeded sarcasm from our benefactors, we settled in for another 24 hours.

Breakfast consisted of chili beans from a pouch and caribou steak. Afterwards, we pulled down the blood-stained tarp used for a wind break and re-erected it as a shelter to sleep under. We used the stakes for the former tent as they were set, since they could not be pulled from the frozen ground by a strong elephant. The tent remnants were fashioned into another windbreak around the cooking area. This finished, we took turns napping under the tarp for two hour intervals while the other kept watch with a rifle at hand. After Reuben's first watch, he reported seeing a single cow caribou, followed at an interval of five minutes, by two wolves. She appeared to be intent on following the trail through our camp but detoured along the east side of the lake when she saw our blue tarp-tent flapping in the wind. We kept to the two-on and two-off schedule throughout the day and ensuing night without any events worthy of note.

The next morning, and we hoped it was our last, we measured the ice thickness first thing; it was between seven and eight inches. The ice was covered by four inches of granular snow, visibility was quite good and a light breeze was blowing out of the south. We reported these details to our friends in Bettles and they told us "Pack up your camp, a plane will come for you in three hours.

It is amazing how a griz visit can disrupt a simple camp. It took every bit of three hours to collect our scattered gear and trash and pack it up for transport. When we finished, the site was almost as pristine as when we arrived except for those damned, immovable tent stakes. We hid them under the snow.

We could hear the De Havilland Beaver before we could see it. Frank circled the lake twice before he set her down on skis, generating an impressive plume of ice and snow, and we began the tedious job of loading meat, antlers, gear and trash. The return ride followed the same route as our outward-bound flight but the country looked very different under its blanket of snow. I saw a small herd of caribou, well-defined against the glaring white, trooping south. I looked for griz, of course, but was disappointed. I enjoy seeing them from 1,000 feet but not much closer.

At Bettles, we booked the bunkhouse, enjoyed a hot shower as only really cold, dirty men can, and had a decent hot meal that was not eaten in wind and snow.   The remainder of the day and most of the next were devoted to the tedious process of boning our meat and packing it in vacuum-sealed bags. We donated one of our hind legs to a nearby Indian village which, from the load their truck carried, made a good haul of caribou and moose, courtesy of the sport hunters. In Fairbanks, we purchased dry ice to keep our meat frozen, dropped off our hides with a local taxidermist for tanning and headed for the southland. The drive back to Seattle was interesting but, uneventful.

Naturally, we had to modify this tale for our wives to exclude dealings with bears and include a fictional fall on the ice to explain the gash on Reuben's forehead. Yes, these amounted to lies, small ones, in the service of humanity or, at least, a small part of it. In the end, both old geologists were satisfied with their arctic adventure and, of course, were gratified that neither of us were making the return trip by air freight in a freezer box.

GROTTO OF THE GOLDEN SNAKE

Ju-long, an 80-something-year-old ethnic Chinese gentleman, raised himself from early childhood in the waterfront streets and sailor dives of pre-war Yokosuka, Japan. He had no memory of his parents, he did not know his age precisely, he never attended any school beyond the Oliver Twist Pick-Pocket Academy and he could not speak a single word of Chinese. An old China sailor, who did speak Chinese, once told him the name Ju-long meant "The Power of a Dragon". Ju-long liked this translation and repeated it to anyone who asked about his foreign-sounding name and appearance.

Japanese prejudices against ethnic Chinese are well-known but they did not deter the youthful Ju-long from growing a fine Fu Manchu mustache, a long queue and adopting a Mandarin outfit based on the cheap Republic movie serials of the nineteen forties when yellow peril entertainment was in vogue. This costume, combined with a menacing hatchet and broken English babble about Chinese tongs and dragon's teeth, were quite effective in persuading deadbeats to pay their gambling debts to his bosses. Of course, that was many years ago during Ju-long's strong-arm career and long, long before he settled into his present legitimate business.

In spite of the many obstacles facing him, Ju-long eventually became a rich and influential figure in the Yokosuka underworld by virtue of disciplined work habits, frugal life style, and innate intelligence. With a university education Ju-long might have entered any profession from medicine to nuclear physics but his impoverished circumstances declared otherwise and the lad was forced into street crime to fill his rice bowl. Over a fifty-year career, this intelligent boy grew to manhood and climbed the ladder of crime from lowly artful dodger to a dealer and artisan in fine jewelry. Jewelry and precious metals became his passion, his calling, and the source of his wealth and influence within the Yokosuka crime community.

His shop, known to the world as The Grotto of the Golden Snake, was a more or less legitimate business by the time of this story and located on a narrow, poorly-lighted, back street with hideous, foul-smelling gutters that backed up with frequency. From the roof of the Golden Snake, Ju-long could, with some difficulty, see the Womble Gate of the U. S. Naval Shipyard, one of three gates that controlled access to the 579-acre restricted peninsula. From this same vantage he could quite easily see the glowing golden arches of McDonald's restaurant on the naval base and, with a little more difficulty, he could also see a portion of the campuses of Mikasa Kindergarten, Shonan Junior College, and the Kanagawa Ladies Dental College; all, of course, well-known attractions to visitors of Yokosuka.

During his long life, Ju-long had witnessed great changes in the part of Yokosuka where he lived and worked. When he was very young, this same naval yard was the beating heart of the vast and powerful Japanese Imperial Navy but by the end of the war it was a smoldering inferno of what was, or might have been. But, from these same ruins, arose a phoenix in the form of what is now the thriving home of the U. S. Seventh Fleet; a model of modern American life, administered and governed by Americans, policed by Americans, and hermetically isolated from the people of Yokosuka, Japanese culture and language.

The Grotto of the Golden Snake was a long, narrow, two-story edifice with bars over both the door and the single external widow at ground level. A sign, swinging over the doorway, proclaimed the name of the shop in both Japanese and English. Naturally, this sign featured a realistic cobra with flared hood, poised and ready to strike, but this snake was composed of cheap brass, rather than gold, in deference to the reduced economic circumstances of the neighborhood. Not that there were many locals who would contemplate stealing from Ju-long; his underworld connections were known to all and made such an idea almost the equivalent of suicide.

Ju-long lived alone above his shop under extremely Spartan conditions; a simple pallet bed, an electric hot plate for boiling tea and rice, a bucket of potable water for cooking and washing, and another bucket for the body functions. This penurious life style was not dictated by financial necessity because Ju-long could afford to live wherever, and however, he wished. But he chose to live in this manner simply because he could not bear to be more than a few steps distance from his shop, his tools and the objects he loved.

From the front door, the shop offered a single narrow passage between floor-to-ceiling shelves of jewelry, watches, and insanely ticking clocks of all sorts and sizes. These goods were arranged to become systematically more expensive as one approached a barred cage at the rear of the building. The cheaper goods were much in demand by U. S. sailors who comprised the majority of Ju-long's customers.

Within the cage, the work benches presented the patron with an astonishingly disordered riot of trays, boxes and jars of tiny parts scattered amidst torches, furnaces, metal cutting tools, drills, bits, dies and clocks in mid-repair. All these were essential to the jewelry trade, certainly, but it was fortunate that these tools were speechless and without memory.

Only Ju-long was permitted behind this cage and he remained there during business hours and often long into the night making repairs or constructing custom jewelry pieces in demand by the socially elite ladies of Yokosuka. Old Ju-long did not require much sleep and never wearied of his claustrophobic surroundings; they reminded him daily of his difficult odyssey from starving, abandoned foundling, forced to shit in public streets, to the respectable, or let us at least say, semi-respectable, business man and artisan that he now was.

Behind this cage, Ju-log was normally occupied with his work. He would almost invariably be found wearing a magnifying jeweler's visor tilted above his regular old-fashioned rimless spectacles. But, at one end of the cage, there was a secret, securely-locked, steel door leading to a fire-proof vault where gold, silver, and platinum bullion were stored along with very expensive jewelry items and diamonds both cut and un-cut. This was Ju-long's real wealth and no one was ever permitted to know of its existence.

Donald Atkins was an alcoholic, former navy man, and American ex-pat, who had lived in Yokosuka for nearly 30 years. When he emerged from the soup kitchen entrance, darkness was beginning to fall over the great city. He had wrapped the heavy white bag in a newspaper and placed it securely in the inside pocket of his pea jacket. Donald considered crossing the street and having a drink or two at the Shit Kicker's Bar but he realized that he needed to be in top mental shape in order to deal with old Ju-long. He had negotiated with this wily master jeweler many times in the past but tonight, tonight he needed Ju-long's advice in a bad way. That old chink bastard knew everything there was to know about gems and precious metals but he was justly infamous for screwing sailors, including Donald himself, out of their last yen.

Donald had formerly been into small-time burglary and, in those days, the old Chinaman fenced practically any type of stolen property, so they were former business associates in a way. Both had been on the straight and narrow for the past few years but they certainly shared many secrets that would interest the Yokosuka police.

Donald simply had to know what was in his white bag that

was worth the lives of two murdered sailors and yet was not gold. He walked at a steady pace but took an indirect route to the Chinaman's seedy shop and paused several times to study the street behind him. He saw only the normal crowd of pedestrians rushing along their various ways toward home and dinner.

Standing before the barred door of the Golden Snake, Donald could make out a faint light coming from the cage in the rear. He pushed the buzzer with three short pulses, then a five second delay, then one extended buzz. It was the secret signal between brothers in crime and Donald had to smile as he recalled just how many times he had made this signal when bringing stolen goods to master jeweler, Ju-long.

Ju-long knew from the buzzer signal that one of his former criminal associates was at his door. A hidden camera, with its lens coincident with the eye of the cobra on his shop sign, informed him that his visitor was one Donald Atkins, formerly of the U. S. Navy, and person of interest to detectives of the Yokosuka police force. He had dealt with Mr. Atkins on many prior occasions and found him to be a reliable master of ignorance but, otherwise, as honestly dishonest as most of the petty criminals he dealt with. He pushed a button that released the lock of the barred front door.

"Good evening, Mr. Atkins" smiled Ju-long with a token bow which could only be taken as an obvious imitation of Hollywood's Charlie Chan. "What brings honorable Navy man to humble Grotto of Golden Snake?"

"Hello Ju-long, it has been a long time since I was last here.

You screwed me on five watches I brought to you, as I recall."

"That was only business, Donald, I am pleased to receive my old friend. The street tells me that you are honest man these days, a soup entrepreneur, and in partnership with the beautiful Ayami Watanabe."

"Yes, and that woman treats me like a god-damned slave when I am ashore; my only escape is shipping out on merchant cruises. In fact, that's why I came to see you, old friend. I picked up something on my last cruise and I need your help in figuring out its value. Don't worry, I am not here to sell or pawn any of my belongings, you old wharf rat." With this, Atkins pulled the parcel from his coat and removed the newspaper wrapping. "It is a heavy metal of some kind, but not gold. I know it is valuable but I need to know what it is to figure what to do with it."

Ju-long eyed the cotton bag on the counter from behind the cage but did not reach for it. Years of experience with sailors had taught him to never exhibit interest in the items they brought in; reluctance was always the best policy, especially if a valuable article was in play. "It seems you have a cotton bag of the type miners often use for storing their ores. I have no interest in such bags."

"God damn it, Ju-long, it's not the bag I want to know about; it's what's in the fucking bag. Open it and tell me what you think" responded Donald with rising heat.

Ju-long, of course, realized he already had the upper hand if there was to be a negotiation between himself and this sailor. He knew very well that he was sitting across the bars from a loser at the top of his game, a loser borne under the well-known brown star.

Atkins pushed the bag through the slot beneath the bars and impatiently waited for the Chinaman to pick it up. Ju-long delayed about 30 seconds and then finally picked up the bag with an obsequious smile and said "Yes, very heavy, very heavy" resuming his Charlie Chan imitation. He then reached back to a work bench and retrieved a pair of needle-nosed pliers. "Shall we open bag and examine contents, Donald?"

"Yes, of course, you have to look at it to tell me what it is, old man" replied Atkins who was growing more and more exasperated with the deliberate pace of the elderly master jeweler who was demonstrating less interest in his bag than watching a street dog shit.

Ju-long used the pliers to meticulously unwrap the wire and opened the bag at last. He directed an intense beam of light from his jeweler's visor into the contents. "Hmmm, yes, very interesting, you have some kind of black sand, Donald, not gold or silver, not brass or bronze, not tin or copper. Definitely back sand, Donald."

"What the hell do you mean by black sand? What is it and how much is it worth?" cried Donald in a voice that clearly betrayed growing irritation.

Ju-long had already guessed from the heft of the bag that it contained platinum concentrate but he was enjoying the sport of playing with this big American fish. "Did you know, Donald, that someone has covered these sand grains with powdered graphite?"

"Yes, I did know it, you old scoundrel, because I did it myself to get the goods past customs if they decided to search my sea bag. Now please Ju-long, let's get on with it" the sailor pleaded, making an obvious effort to calm himself. The old Chinaman always pulled this shit, getting a guy so pissed-off that he couldn't keep his eye on the ball.

"I am truly sorry if I upset you, Donald, but you cannot expect an old man to identify an unknown mystery material with a single brief glance. Permit me to make a crude calculation of the density of this black sand. It may resolve the mystery." With this, he resealed the bag leaving a single pea-sized grain on the table. He mashed this grain with a small hammer and quickly passed a pen magnet over it which attracted the flattened grain. Then he weighed the bag on a nearby scale; it was exactly 4500 grams or 4.5 kilograms. Next, the jeweler measured the length of the bag at 15 centimeters and then rolled the bag between his hands into a cylinder with a circular cross-section from which he measured a diameter of five centimeters. The nervous sailor followed these proceeding in a nearly hypnotic state.

Ju-long then retrieved an antique Chinese abacus from behind the counter and began clicking beads, this way and that, in very rapid succession. Ju-long knew how to use a Chinese abacus, not because he was ethnic Chinese, but because he had studied a book on the subject for over a year. This abacus routine was an exhibition the jeweler very much enjoyed presenting because the stupid sailors watching it were always completely bedazzled and impressed. Besides, in the hands of an expert, it was as accurate and fast as any modern electronic calculator when it came to arithmetic operations. In less than 10 seconds, Ju-long said "The volume of a cylinder with the dimensions we measured is 294.52 cubic centimeters but this must be reduced by 25 % to account for open spaces between the sand grains. Thus, the approximate volume of the metal grains is ..." here he paused and batted more beads along the abacus wires while noting the zombie-like expression on Atkins' face ... "ah yes, the corrected volume is 220.89 cubic centimeters. Now we compute a crude density value by dividing the mass of 4500 by the corrected volume of 220.89 and arrive at estimated density of 20.3 grams per cubic centimeter. Did you follow that calculation, Donald?"

"Fuck no, I didn't follow that calculation. Who the hell could understand all this Chinese mumbo-jumbo mathematical bull shit? Just tell me what it means before I come into that cage and pull your arms and legs off."

Ju-long smiled, within himself, of course, he had taken Mr. Atkins as far as he could, just short of violence, so he said in a soothing, obsequiously polite, Charlie Chan manner "Why Donald, this means you are rich man because bag contains high-grade platinum ore."

"It's platinum? God damn it, Ju-long, you are alright! I am fucking rich!" Donald cried out in an ecstasy of greed. "Quick, tell me what it is worth, Ju-long!"

"This is not so easy, my son, because assumptions have to be made as to the percentage of platinum in the ore and the market price of the platinum which changes all the time. Then there are the other platinum group elements which we cannot evaluate without an assay" responded the jeweler with a cunning twinkle in his eyes that was shielded from the now happy ex-sailor by the visor.

"Ok, ok, I get that, Ju-long, but you can give me a rough estimate, can't you?" begged Atkins.

"Yes, yes, a very rough estimate of the *intrinsic* value of the platinum alone if you wish it" and Ju-long picked up the abacus and repeated his previous routine. "In what currency do you wish to express the value, Donald, Japanese yen or Hong Kong dollars?"

"Jesus Christ, Ju-long, cut the horse shit and tell me what the sack is worth in U. S. dollars."

There were additional bead movements designed to increase Donald's agony but, at length, Ju-long relented and said "The *intrinsic* value is something in neighborhood of 180,000 U. S. dollars."

Donald Atkins sat in awed silence for once. This was an astronomical number as far as he was concerned, far, far beyond his greediest speculations, and he was already regretting that he had not stolen a second bag, or even a third, when he had the opportunity.

"I sense this is welcome news for you, Donald, but at the same time I fear there is also some bad news" said the old Chinaman, now in a sincere and gentle tone.

"What the hell can be bad about a 180 thousand bucks, Ju-long?" the now smiling sailor quipped in joyful response

"Just this, Donald, to get money for your platinum ore it must be refined to a state of purity, to what is called 'fine platinum'. Only then can it be traded commercially and you will not be able to have such a small amount of ore refined by any commercial refinery. A small private laboratory, perhaps one affiliated with the dental industry, might be persuaded to do the job but they will charge a significant commission for this service. I have heard that Fugimora Precious Metals does such small jobs but, perhaps, you do not wish to deal with Fugimora Industries."

At this, the expression on the sailor's face changed from radiant to something approaching cadaverous. His color became sickly grey and he swallowed hard several times causing his Adam's apple to bob in a ridiculous way. He could not speak for a few moments, but at last croaked out "Fugimora Industries? No, no, I can't do that at all, it is impossible because it's their platinum we are looking at!"

"Ah, yes, I thought as much, Donald. This compounds your difficulties, my son, as the Fugimora clan will certainly be looking for you and they will be very insistent for the return of their property; very insistent. I trust you follow my meaning, Donald."

"Jesus Fucking Christ, Ju-long, are you are telling me I can't sell it, I can't keep it, and either way the Fugimora's want to kill me?"

"I am afraid that is my view of your situation, Donald. I do not know what you can do except return their property and pray for mercy. As the matter stands, you are a walking corpse and, that is merely a temporary state."

At this point, former seaman Donald Atkins was at least on familiar ground, the ground tread by losers; a place from which there is no path to redemption. He needed to think, he needed a plan and, most of all, he needed to get drunk. He snatched the bag off the table and thrust it back into the inside pocket of his coat. He stared wildly at the inscrutable face of Ju-long behind the cage in his rimless spectacles and jeweler visor. "You have been a big fucking help, you crooked old bastard. Thanks a-fucking-lot. Now buzz me out!" He rose from his stool and raced to the door. When the lock released, he peered out the doorway into the Yokosuka darkness and looked keenly in every direction. He saw people, of course, but he saw no one who looked like an assassin and no one who resembled Ryota Fugimora, the man he had stolen from on the Fugimora ship, *Aoki Maru*.

Ryota Fugimora had no difficulty following a six foot two-inch-tall Caucasian with blonde hair through the narrow streets of the waterfront district to the door of The Grotto of the Golden Snake. Fugimora was not familiar with Ju-long, his establishment or his underworld reputation but it did not require a brain surgeon to deduce the business being conducted through the cage at the rear of that building.

Donald Atkins walked rapidly, thinking only about the first drink he would have at the Shit Kicker's Bar. After two blocks, he mechanically stopped and looked back over his shoulder along his route from the Golden Snake. A shock, like that delivered by the electric chair, pulsed though every part of his body, momentarily paralyzing him.

It just could not be, it must be an alcoholic nightmare, life could not possibly end in such a fucked up way. Yet...there he was! He was standing just twenty yards away, dressed in black like some fucking Samurai warrior with a sadistic, grim expression on his ugly, yellow, oriental face. He knew this face. He feared this face. He had good reason for this fear, it was the monstrously impassive face of Ryota Fugimora.

Ryota watched calmly as sailor Atkins plummeted into a state of unthinking, raw terror and then began running blindly down the street. Fugimora was enough of a hunter to know that a rabbit in full panic mode will soon make a fatal mistake. He did not bother to run after the fleeing 61-year-old sailor, he merely pursued him at a normal walking pace keeping his elongate bundle securely under his arm.

Atkins turned right into the first narrow alley he came to and raced through the darkness amidst litter, overflowing garbage cans and scurrying rats. Ryota paused at the entrance to this alley and very nearly broke into an actual smile which would have been an extreme rarity for this misanthropic young man. At eye level, there was a sign in Japanese warning pedestrians and cyclists that this was a blind alley. But, of course, he knew that Donald Atkins could not read Japanese.

Donald ran as he had never run in his life. Thank God he was wearing his athletic shoes instead of his clunky seaman shoes but he was getting a stitch in his side and his lungs were on fire. The dead weight of the 4.5-kilogram bag in his coat felt like an anchor; he retrieved it and found its weight repulsive; the bag now seemed abhorrent and odious to his soul. It was like holding a hideous, writhing snake and he realized, in this moment of peril, that his black sand was a worthless, filthy, vacuous thing; an evil mass that was not at all worth dying for. He flung it wildly aside into one of the hundreds of seething, rat-filled cans of garbage as he flew past. He immediately felt lighter, faster, almost like a better man.

He ran now with abandon; he ran for absolution for a poorly-lived life; he ran for the fragrant flower of life itself. He knew he was increasing the distance between himself and the man in black and now, if there could just be a crossing alley that he could turn into, then perhaps, escape would be possible. But there were no crossing alleys and the alley he was confined in terminated 20 yards straight ahead of him with a crazy, disorganized stack of garbage cans. The race of races was over and he knew it. Christ, he knew it.

Ryota Fugimora walked steadily and, of course, without emotion. He knew what he would find at the alley's end. At 30-yards distance from this dead end he drew a 400-year-old samurai sword from his bundle and dropped the sheath and covering to the pavement.

Donald waited at the extreme corner of the alley, gasping audibly, trembling uncontrollably and wielding the lid of a garbage can defensively. Ryota closed the distance separating them and assumed the offensive crouching position of the Samurai warrior with the two-handed sword held horizontally over his right shoulder. Then, with a sudden, unexpected, catlike leap, Fugimora reduced the intervening distance to one meter and made a feinting stab at the sailor's torso causing Donald to lower his shield in response. In true Samurai fashion this feint was followed by a swift horizontal slash at neck level and, in a fraction of a second, the head of sailor Donald Atkins was spinning away into the darkness and filth of a Yokosuka waterfront alley.

Ryota calmly restrained each arm of the twitching corpse with his foot and deftly removed both hands with a single cut for each. The severed appendages and head were placed in a rubber bag carried expressly for this purpose. He then wiped the long, gleaming blade on Donald's pea coat and thoroughly searched through the clothing of the dead man. Ryota did not find the all-important white bag, but the young killer did not particularly care about the monetary value of this loss; no, his concern was that this black sand was a dangling thread that, if pulled, could unravel the fabric of the Fugimora wheel of fortune.

HA'BOON

In the year 2025, a juvenile male baboon, named Reginald, arrived at the home of Harry Borden at 1:30 a.m. The agent of Acme Live Delivery rang the bell persistently and, at length, the door was opened by Mr. Harry, himself. Harry was balding, had an enormous paunch, a grotesque double chin and he was drunk. He was a sick man, a spiteful man, an unattractive man, and he believed his liver was diseased.

Music, emanating from the darkened interior, blared behind Harry, and this not just at the Borden residence, but all down this street, and nearly every other street in the city, where raucous parties were in progress. These parties would go on until daylight in neighborhoods all across Omaha. Do not picture the sedate dinner parties of yesteryear, but rather, wild, tempestuous affairs featuring an abundance of multi-colored pills, alcohol, marijuana, wife-swapping and dangerously loud music.

"Ha'boon?" uttered Mr. Borden as he blinked in the unaccustomed brightness of his porch light. This relatively new American colloquialism was the disgraceful contraction of "how is your baboon?"; it had swept the country like the zika virus during the last three years.

The delivery man dutifully replied "Ha'boon?" followed by "I got a live male booney for ya mister, where ya want me to put him?"

Mr. Borden directed the Acme Live Delivery man to place the crate containing the creature in his temperature-controlled basement which now served as home and prison for his adopted baboons. The concrete room was painted institutional green; it was windowless and featureless, like a hospital waiting room without the ornate diplomas and smiling photos of the attending physicians. A ring of keys, heavy leather gauntlets, plastic clench ties and an anesthetizing dart-gun hung on the wall nearest the door; a small, collapsible stretcher leaned ominously in a corner. The barred cages, themselves, were elaborate affairs measuring 6 by 8 by 6 feet and featured small hammocks, automatic watering spouts, feed bins and bars and rings meant for exercise. These confining structures were mounted on legs 12 inches above a wide floor-tray filled with wood shavings that provided for daily waste clean-up by an attendant. A rotating camera, mounted to the ceiling kept Mr. Harry apprised of the status of his wards around the clock.

Lester, the long-time resident male baboon, sat glumly in his cage and did not look up or acknowledge the arrival of his brother baboon. He was wise enough to understand that this new arrival marked the end of his tenure and its implications. This was the ultimate indicator that he would be scheduled for surgery in the near future. Poor Lester realized that he would soon be the unwilling donor of Mr. Harry's new liver and, perhaps heart and lungs as well. For the past few weeks, Lester had been in deep consternation of the abuse Mr. Borden was inflicting upon himself.

The original human liver had been taking a beating for some time as a result of Mr. Borden's excessive lifestyle, which had evolved to one of total dissipation.

Lester examined Mr. Harry's eyes whenever chance permitted, they were always red from drinking, but he knew they would soon enough become yellow and that would signal the end for Lester the baboon.

Borden, like his hard-partying neighbors, could afford the price of a healthy baboon as well as the cost of elective surgery. Baboons are now widely raised in confinement across the USA and selectively bred for size and passivity in so-called "booney mills" which now prospered just beyond the suburbs of every major city in the country.

Because of their close approach to human DNA, chimpanzees were the initial choice as organ donors, and this was quite successful from the medical perspective. But their lovable, human-like traits and gift for mimicry quickly sparked moral outrage by animal-rights advocates and laws protecting chimps were soon enacted. Besides, by endearing themselves to their human masters, they soon became enthusiastic partners in the outrageous behavior which created the need for organ replacement. As a result, wealthy, loving chimp-masters were soon faced with the unexpected burden of replacing their pet chimp's vital organs as well as their own.

Initially, such dissipated chimps were rejuvenated with baboon organs and, eventually, this led to the revelation that these same organs could be just as successfully transplanted into humans, eliminating the sacrifice of chimps on the altar of medical expediency. Of course, baboons are completely lacking in endearing traits and their doglike muzzles, bone-crushing jaws, formidable fighting fangs and nasty habits are quite repulsive to humans. Predictably, animal-rights people had no issues at all with industrial-scale harvesting of baboon organs.

Think of it... all the liquor, tobacco, drugs and unprotected sex you care to indulge in without consequence! All thanks to advances in robotic microsurgery and a $30 per hour minimum wage for the working class. Sin, tidal waves of it, became the order of the day at all social levels, doctors, lawyers, professors, office workers, tradesmen and even garbage collectors. Perhaps predictably, these medical advances resulted in unforeseen negative consequences in the social behavior of the upper and middle classes who could afford to keep live animal donors. The poorer classes, in contrast, were forced to accept dribble-down harvested organs which sell at discount in a market where medical advances permit transplantation of any baboon organ to humans without fear of rejection or infection. In this dystopian environment, demand for human organs, all of which are now suspect, is lower than that of leprous armadillo organs. What a country!

Every pocket mall in the prosperous parts of cities, coast to coast, now boasts of 24-hour emergency medical clinics, board-certified for transplant procedures with blazing neon signs proclaiming *"We specialize in lung-liver-heart transplants/easy terms/no payment for 1 year"*. These clinics offer harvested frozen baboon parts at greatly discounted prices relative to the purchase and maintenance cost of a living, young, healthy booney.

The wealthy, naturally, prefer to raise their own baboons to insure healthy organs and immediate availability and often elect to have several organs transplanted in a single surgical intervention. Those organs not required by the human owner are wholesaled to the insatiable 24-hour-clinics, thereby reducing costs of the procedure.

Farmers, in 2025, now augment their income from food crops and traditional livestock by raising baboons. Purina, of course, makes a specially formulated, healthy baboon chow for this booming market. The favored donor-species is *Papio ursinas,* originating in the Cape region of South Africa. They are commonly called chacina baboons, the largest of the five-baboon species, and for this reason are optimal donors. Would you believe that the current chacina population in the USA now exceeds that of the entire African Continent?

People, both men and women, in the time of this story, are totally obsessed with youth preservation, revivification through plastic surgery and replacement of organs damaged through personal excess. Any organ, except the brain, of course, is available; yes, even penises, testicles, and ovaries, although, thus far, no one has publicly admitted to electing these particular procedures. One may wonder what level of extremity would drive a man to request a baboon penis but, perhaps, certain combat and fire injuries would qualify. All of these elective procedures are recommended on TV by attractive older couples, paid actors who, convincingly, swear they function better than the original equipment and produce no traces of simian behavior. These advertisements suggest, without explicitly stating, that the couples are still sexually active.

Mr. Harry Borden hobbled on his cane into the basement room housing his baboon wards. It was 2:30 p.m., and he was enjoying a severe attack of gout in his right great toe, a debilitating hangover and the effects of only four hours of sleep. His daily "eye-opener", a large bloody Mary with a stalk of celery, was half consumed. He set his drink down and pushed the crate containing Reginald up against the empty cage so that the doors of the two structures more or less coincided and then raised the sliding gates of each with a stick kept for that purpose.

Reginald was frightened and disoriented, of course, and he did not wish to move into his new home. Mr. Harry encouraged him by prodding with his stick and, after some effort, the exchange was made. Reginald retreated to the farthest corner of his new home and silently glowered at his new master. This trivial exertion was sufficient to exhaust the suffering Mr. Harry, so he picked up his drink, downed the remains in three practiced gulps, threw his prodding stick on top of the packing crate and retreated upstairs to the siren call of his liquor cabinet.

Primate researchers tell us that baboons are omnivorous

creatures and possess at least 10 vocalizations to communicate with each other. This means there is a simple language for baboons. Actually, the true number of such vocalizations is closer to 50 than 10. This underestimation is due to the inability of researchers to distinguish subtle tonal differences and hand gestures in this simian language. Just as importantly, baboons have opposable thumbs, like all Old-World monkeys, and short tails rather than the long, prehensile appendages of monkeys. Beyond this, we must note that baboons are excellent climbers and swimmers, have thick fur which changes from brown to grey with maturity and exhibit excellent binocular and stereoscopic vision due to close-set, forward-looking eyes with amber irises and black pupils. In terms of reproduction, gestation is 183 days and usually produces one infant which is weaned at one year. Juvenile baboons reach sexual maturity at an age between five and eight years.

The question of intelligence is more difficult to assess. Primatologists tell us that baboons have a larger brain-to-body mass ratio than chimpanzees which, everyone knows, demonstrate remarkable learning skills. Evidently, this is the result of baboon adaptation to savannah life, as was the case of primitive humans, whereas chimps remained forest dwellers. Experiments have shown that baboons are quite capable of simple numerical discrimination. Like human children, they know the difference between 2 peanuts and 8 peanuts but not between 9 and 10 peanuts.

The average baboon brain has a mass of about 140 grams and an average body weight of about 30 kilograms; this leads to a brain-to-body mass ratio of 0.0047. This is a small number, if compared with humans whose average brain-to-body mass ratio is 0.0226. This comparison suggests that humans are smarter than baboons by a factor of nearly 5.0. It certainly means that baboons will not be discussing quantum mechanics in their basement cages, but they are far from stupid.

Lester had remained impassive during the installation of Reginald into his new home but, the instant Mr. Harry departed, he sprang into activity by speaking to the new arrival. Formal introductions were made and Lester explained the purpose behind their captivity in this basement prison. It is fair to say that the naïve, half-grown Reginald was shocked to learn what his future was to be in the Borden household. Poor Reggie was a third generation rural-booney, raised on an isolated farm 12 miles outside of Chadron, Nebraska, and he was poorly informed about the facts of life in the big city.

Lester gently informed the youngster that, unless they contrived a method of escape, their fate was premature death on an operating table adjacent to their master, Mr. Harry. This message had to be repeated several times before it could be understood by the younger baboon whose linguistic skills were not fully developed. Lester had watched the transfer process very carefully, particularly the position where Borden had left the prodding stick. It was the first mistake the master had ever made, no doubt a result of declining health. But now, it was within reach of Reginald's cage!

Lester explained, in as much detail as baboon language permitted, that Reggie should reach through the bars and seize the stick, touch it to the floor where sticky packing tape, sealing the door of the wooden shipping box, lay. He was then to hand the stick through the bars to Lester. By issuing instructions, one simple step at a time, Reggie was able to hand the prodding stick with a foot-long piece of tape on the end across the space separating their cages. Reggie was mystified by this procedure but the much wiser Lester was already calculating an escape plan.

It was a simple matter for Lester to attach the tape securely to the end of the stick and reach out with it to the key ring on the wall. With keys in hand, it was an easy maneuver for the older baboon to unlock his cage and return the keys to their original position and instruct Reginald to replace the stick to its former position on the packing crate. Of course, these forbidden actions were duly recorded by the all-seeing ceiling camera, but Mr. Harry had long ago given up the practice of reviewing the recorded tapes which were automatically erased every 24 hours. In fact, he had practically forgotten the presence of the camera.

That evening followed the general routine for the Borden household, meaning that guests in the early stages of drunkeness began arriving around 7 p.m. These were mostly the younger crowd who lived in apartments, could not afford to host parties themselves and, because they were still immortal, had no thoughts of baboons or life-saving organ transplants. By 9 p.m., older guests began arriving in more advanced stages of inebriation. These individuals, both men and women, had every reason to utter the greeting "Ha'boon?" and mean it sincerely. For them, there were no illusions about immortality.

Lester waited with the patience of a hunter for the party to reach its crescendo which experience had taught him would occur about 1 a.m. He advised Reggie to eat as much food and drink as much water as he could sustain because they could not know when they would get their next meal. By midnight, the chaos above the basement was in full swing, laughter, shrieks, loud music, clouds of smoke, and couples sneaking off to bedrooms and closets for meaningless sex. It was a routine quite familiar to the older baboon.

At about 12:30 a.m., Lester judged the moment right for escape and carefully opened the door of his cage, fetched the key ring and opened Reggie's cage. He then locked both cages and returned the ring to its hook in the wall. This unnecessary move was the product of baboon intelligence, a symbolic blow for animal justice and an intentional personal insult to Mr. Harry.

The access door to the baboon room was never locked, so the escapees had only to pass the foot of the stairs leading up the house proper and open the back door leading to freedom. They witnessed two people at the top of the stairway engaged in oral sex but the couple did not notice the furtive baboons.

The fences that enclose all suburban back yards is a freeway for squirrels, cats and, in this instance, baboons and the fleeing pair were soon miles from the Borden house. Lester led the team in an easterly direction, guided by the scent of the Missouri River which lay in that direction. He did not know why he chose this path, he had no conscious memory of any geographic features of the great city, but instinct and the odors reaching his brain assured him that this was the right direction. The pair travelled at a rapid pace along almost continuous fences and crossed the road intersections with extreme caution but there was very little traffic at this hour because of the ubiquitous parties in progress. When morning broke, they were close enough to the river to hear the engines of tow boats and smell their diesel fumes.

Lester picked a tall, leafy cottonwood tree and they both found a comfortable crotch in the limbs and went to sleep. About mid-day they were awakened by a growling dog at the base of their tree and Lester climbed down to a lower limb, just out of reach of the dog, and let off the most hideous hissing snarl ever heard by a canine accompanied by an exhibition of his fearsome fighting fangs. The poor dog was entirely intimidated and retreated whimpering back to his home. The dog did not return and the remaining daylight hours passed restfully for the escapees.

The nocturnal, cross-city traverse of the fleeing baboons had followed a course along alley ways parallel to the busy Harrison Street in southeast Omaha up to the point where further progress was blocked by Interstate 75. The Harrison Street underpass, beneath I-75, was open to traffic around the clock but there were indigent humans squatting along it's margins and the fugitive pair were forced to wait until 3:30 a.m. before the last of these unhappy residents retired to their miserable abodes. The baboons crept, carefully, through the debris of poverty, shopping carts, trash-can fires, cardboard huts, tents, liquor bottles, human excrement and every variety of refuse derived from this life style, to the other side of I-75. They skirted the Southroads Mall on Bellevue Boulevard and headed directly for the safety of the Fontenelle Forest.

This forest land, measuring about four by two miles in area, occupied a meander loop in the Missouri River and enclosed no human dwellings, businesses or roads. It was perfect for two baboons fleeing transplant surgery. But…there was a scent in the air of this forest, a strange and unexpected scent, the scent of baboons, many baboons. This scent grew stronger as Lester and Reggie penetrated deeper into the forest and closer to the river. At last, Lester called a halt to their journey and squatted submissively in the middle of a small clearing of the trees. His nose told him they were now surrounded by a troop of baboons. The travelers remained in position, making no sounds or gestures for nearly thirty minutes before a single, quite elderly, grey male baboon made his presence known by approaching them from the trees.

Lester, recognizing both the danger and solemnity of the situation, spoke out "Greetings, O Wise One, we come in peace seeking sanctuary from the human butchers".

"Aye, this is understood" replied the old one "We all have sought this forest refuge for this same reason. We rule these woods and you are welcome to our society but we have rules here. Very harsh rules. No baboon may show himself to humans, ever, on pain of death for both the human and the offender. This means no daylight activity, you both must become, like us, creatures of the night and remain hidden during the day. We realize that this rule for nocturnal and arboreal life is counter to the normal life style of baboons, but we are surrounded by uncountable numbers of human enemies and they have terrible sleep-guns that reach up into the tallest trees to capture us".

Lester, understanding the veiled threat, replied to the king baboon "Yes, we bow to your authority, we understand and accept your death-rule. I myself have beheld the sleep-gun of my former master, I know of its purpose and danger".

"Very well, newcomers, I must call in the troop that they may learn your scent and that you are accepted as members of our group" and he gave a bark that brought the entire pack of 40 or 50 males and females out of the undergrowth. They passed single-file by Lester and Reggie taking in their scent and meeting their eyes directly. When this silent ritual was completed, the king said "The sun will soon rise so we must all be off to our hiding places. You and the youngster will stay with me until you find your own place of safety".

Lester and Reggie followed the elderly baboon at a respectful distance into the dense woods and, ultimately, to a narrow crevice between two large rocks. The king slid adroitly into this opening, Reggie followed but Lester, being the largest of the three, had difficulty and just managed to scrap through the aperture leaving some of his fur behind. The interior was dark, but spacious, and there were piles of dry leaves to serve as bedding. The baboon king offered them water dripping down through fracture in the overhead rock and some dried fruit. Before they went to their beds, the elderly king, speaking aside to Lester, said "You must be certain that your young friend understands the concept of death. I find that youngsters of our kind often do not".

"Yes, Wise One, I will do this, but may I ask why you have not led your troop to the city zoo, surely the baboon yard there is a safer place than here in the woods where we can be hunted by the humans."

"I see you are a perceptive baboon, Lester, but the truth is that the zoo is the worst place for us. The keepers are completely corrupt and under control of the humans behind the baboon market. They steal the baby baboons from their mothers and sell them, they sell any animals they catch trying to escape or enter the zoo property. They sell newly arrived baboons while they are in quarantine. They are the very worst of our human enemies, and I should know because I was an inmate of the Henry Doorly Zoo and Aquarium for several years when I was younger. Believe me, Lester, you do not want to go near that place".

Harry Borden was not happy when he discovered the loss of his baboons, in fact, he flew into a violent rage that very nearly triggered a cardiac event. "How did they do it? Why did they do it? What am I to do now?" He was mystified by the locked cages and the presence of the keys in their accustomed place. He concluded that they must have had human assistance, it had to be one of those god-damn drunken guests, probably screwing in his basement. He called the police and the animal-control people and gave them detailed descriptions of the fugitives. Then he opened a new bottle of vodka and went to the fridge in search of tomato juice.

Mr. Harry, without his living organ bank, was forced to confront his circumstances realistically. The nightly parties stopped, he tried to cut back on his drinking and smoking but found this difficult at his stage of dissipation. He read up on the habits of baboons in the wild. He studied maps of the city obsessively, where could baboons escape human attention in a big city? There could not be that many possibilities. He visited the Henry Doorly Zoo and questioned the baboon keepers intently. They were no help, they claimed there was no change in the population in their care beyond the usual births and deaths. He visited the train and bus stations and even the airports. No one reported baboons lurking about. He knew from his reading that baboons were not creatures of the forest, but they were smart and adaptable and, given no other choice, they could live under forest conditions if the place were isolated from human contact. There was such a place, only one, in Omaha where this was possible, Fontenelle Forest in the southeast part of the city.

Borden spent four consecutive Saturday afternoons wandering around the forest with his eyes glued to the ground searching for baboon dung. Mr. Harry considered himself an expert on baboon dung but his searches ended in failure. Failure, that is, until the last hour of the fourth Saturday, when he found a single, very fresh, baboon turd. It was only one turd, but it enough for the overweight alcoholic, he knew they were here.

That week he placed an ad in the classified section of the Omaha World-Herald seeking baboon hunters and promising a $1000 reward for every baboon caught without injury. He was amazed with the response this reward offer generated, more than 300 men and 13 women responded. He culled his list of candidates down to 100, choosing people who had experience with tranquilizer-dart guns, those with nets for catching animals falling from trees, and men versed in handling baboons.

It was clear to Mr. Harry that the baboons could only avoid human contact by restricting their activities to the nocturnal hours so he devised an elaborate scheme for a night-time search of Fontenelle Forest. At exactly 9 p.m., fifty men would form a line, with a spacing of five yards between individuals, and comb through the woods east to the river with flash lights, dart guns and nets. Any flushed baboons would be trapped by the river. At the river, the men would realign to cut an adjacent swath back through the woods to the west in the direction of the city. Baboons flushed in the westward traverse would be forced into the arms of the fifty hunters waiting there. It would be just like mowing a lawn. Some of the fifty hunters on the western team would respond with stretchers to any point in the forest when a baboon went down.

The captains of both teams were to remain in constant telephone contact. It was a good plan, a masterful plan, but it was a plan that did not account for the sagacity of the elderly baboon king.

The king of the baboons was not only old and wise, he was also a wily strategist and was informed by lookouts when the human hunting party began its initial traverse in Fontenelle Forest. He designated five youthful individuals, among them Reginald, the former ward of Harry Borden, to flee before the hunters, allowing the human to see them in mock-panic. They were to lure the human to river's edge then swim downstream and return to the king's headquarters. The remaining members of the troop were to form up in the rear of the advancing hunters and silently follow them to the river. Then, attack!

The hunters, fifty abreast, advanced through the woods with dart guns at the ready. Their leader, Mr. Harry Borden, was attired in jodhpur trousers, English riding boots, plumed Alpine hat and carried an ornate walking stick with his dart gun slung over one shoulder. With his enormous paunch, he was a ringer for Hermann Göring, *Reichsjägermeister*, of pre-war Nazi Germany, whom he physically resembled. The party marched forward confidently and in good order, their spirits fortified by pocket flasks. Flashlights illuminated the woods eerily, the racket produced could wake the dead.

It was not long before the first baboon was sighted and the orderly procession transformed into a melee of half-drunk men running and shouting in pursuit. More baboons were sighted and the chaos intensified while, silently, the horde of adult baboons closed in behind them. At length, the humans with their darts and nets stood in a clearing on a gravel band of the Missouri River wondering greatly at the absence of their quarry. More than one had recourse to his pocket flask.

Suddenly, in the midst of their perplexity, the humans found themselves surrounded by snarling, enraged baboons, intent on their destruction. Some men jumped into the river, some attempted to engage the baboons, but the more cowardly, including Mr. Harry, slipped through the ranks of the attacking baboons to regain the woods. The hunt master was truly terrified and ran through the dark forest as fast as his chubby legs would carry him, but that was not fast or far.

Borden was forced to stop to relieve the painful thumping of his overworked heart and recharge his lungs. At that moment, a large male baboon dropped from a tree and confronted the wheezing human with radiant eyes and slavering fighting fangs. It was Lester!

Harry recognized his former ward immediately and was struck by how much more intimidating this simian creature appeared without steel bars separating them. Borden's knees turned to jelly, his eyes bulged unnaturally and the coppery taste of fear flooded his mouth. He knew, in this moment, that it was his vital organs that were at risk.

Lester wanted to prolong this exquisite moment, he wanted to play with his former master before making his kill. He issued a horrible snarling growl and feigned a charge with eyes blazing hatred and bone-crushing jaws wide open. Harry, who had lost his dart gun during the chaos, responded by swinging his walking stick like a baseball bat. It was pathetic, and certainly no defense against an angry baboon in his prime. Lester played at feints three more times noting that the stick response was slower and weaker each time.

It was time to end it, to put an end to Mr. Harry Borden and his fantasies of eternal youth and organ transplants. Lester coiled his hind legs and sprang, his powerful hands with those deadly opposable thumbs aimed at the flabby throat of his former master. But it was too late, altogether too late. Harry Borden's diseased heart stopped beating just as Lester's feet left the ground. "Ha'boon?"

THE CORCORAN DREAM

Our heroine, an elderly widow, could positively hear the subtle hiss of air escaping from her new air bed. She tossed, turned and wrestled with the damned thing until nearly midnight before dropping into a fitful sleep. Her initial dreams were inconsequential and frustrating, which is to say typical, until the early morning hours when a recurring dream that she had loved since childhood began to materialize. This dream was in color and had specific smells; she called it "The Corcoran Dream". It had occurred many times in her long life and each time it was exactly the same, immutable, as unchanging as a slab of granite. This dream combined elements of her actual childhood history with elements of fantasy. She liked the fantasy parts best.

It always began with her as a child, perhaps six or seven years old, which would place the year around 1950. She was dressed in a faded blue smock that her mother had made from Gold Medal flour sacking, and she was always barefoot, walking down a dusty dirt road between cotton fields on a simmering August morning, an unknown number of miles outside of Corcoran, California. Haunting melodies of western larks, rudely pierced by inharmonious cries of raucous killdeers, floated across her dream journey. Hot dust squished up between her toes forming little tornados and she could smell the heat, the dust, and even the distinctly metallic odor of the slate-green cotton plants, now displaying their white bolls. Like a tranquil sea, the cotton seemed to extend forever across this flat, featureless farmland, ultimately merging with a cloudless lapis sky.

Corcoran, you should know, was incorporated as a city in Kings County, California in 1914. Nowadays, it is famous for the California State Prison confining the notorious Charles Manson but, in 1950, it was just a small dusty town, hardly more than a village really, of 3100 souls serving the needs of a large and prosperous farm community in the southern San Joaquin Valley. There was no prison then, but there was the basin of the extinct Tulare Lake, a large area of lake sediments of almost fictional fertility and the junction of the San Francisco and San Joaquin Valley Railroads established in 1898. Towns have been founded on less.

Gossypium hirsutum is Latin for money and lots of it, for it is the Linnaean name of the cotton plant native to the New World that was grown on almost every inch of cultivable land surrounding Corcoran in the fifties. Its common name is acala, or upland cotton, and it is immune to the insidious boll weevil that ruined cotton farming in the southern states. Cotton is planted in March and April and harvested by hard-working human pickers or machines in August and September. This introduction of cotton picking machines in California, during the late forties and early fifties, sparked ugly disputes between wealthy farmers and the mostly white labor force of poor, displaced, share-croppers from Oklahoma, Arkansas and Texas. If you have read The Grapes of

Wrath, you will have an idea about this ugliness.

As the dream progressed, a clump of sun flowers at the edge of the dirt road materialized. This marked her favorite part of this dream for she knew that they concealed Harold, the jack rabbit. Harold, she had given him this name decades ago, sat motionless, patiently awaiting her in the shade of sun flowers buzzing with honey bees. She approached close enough to see her own inverted reflection in Harold's large, unblinking black pupils engulfed by handsome yellow-ochre irises. His eyes reminded her of a lovely bowl of Mama's butterscotch pudding with raisins.

Sitting aristocratically on his haunches with ears upright, he was a profile of nobility and nearly as tall as she. She could just discern the slightest twiddling motion of his whiskers as he breathed in the searing air of the breezeless August morning. She thought Harold was so very handsome in his sleek, dark-grey furry coat, posing impassively for her with ears erect. She longed to reach out to Harold and touch him, hug him, and tell him to be wary of boys with .22 rifles. But the dream never allowed her to do this. Immutable. She could never understand why her brothers were always trying to shoot these beautiful creatures and after sixty years she still did not understand this aspect of male behavior. Now, even six decades later, she thought of Harold as still there, sitting stoically amidst his sun flowers, a kind of enchanted rabbit that did not know age or change.

At this point in the dream, a bright-yellow, crop-dusting biplane, issuing a cloudy trail of pesticide, approached her from the distance, flying very low over the endless files of cotton plants. It finally swooped up in a fluid, graceful, looping curve and descended to make another run in the opposite direction. The buzz of the engine and the graceful swoops reminded her of the intricate dancing of bees working flowers in their endless quest for nectar.

Next, the scene of the dream always changed to their temporary home in a shabby worker's bungalow, an empty euphemism for a drafty, unpainted, rodent-infested shack with four lumpy beds and a rusty old wood stove and no plumbing. This gritty hovel, it merited no better name, passed as accommodation for married field workers at $12 a month. Its amenities consisted of a rickety outhouse, two dented 15-gallon galvanized tubs for washing clothes and bathing children, and an outside spigot that issued irrigation water; these luxuries were shared among three other family bungalows. The landowner called this arrangement "family homes with laundry facilities and running water". Can you imagine?

As always in this dream, she saw her mother standing at the stove frying pancakes on a griddle. She could smell the sizzling cakes and strong southern coffee that her mom made for dad and the boys early each morning before they trudged to the fields with their long dirty bags for gathering cotton slung across their shoulders.

Mom always appeared the same, wearing a faded polka-dot house dress, broken down shoes that must have been white at one time, and a dirty white apron. These details never varied. Mom always faced away from her in this dream so she could never see her face, not even once. It took 50 years for her to understand why this should be. She understood it now, now that she was an old lady herself. It was a defense mechanism, one contrived to protect her from seeing the youthful face of her mother when the child that lady had birthed and raised was in her seventies.

She marveled at the fantastic aroma of the pancakes and coffee in this particular episode of the dream, measurably more intense than anything in the past. At last, it was a long-awaited change that she had always yearned for. But then she realized that her eyes were open and she was sitting up in her fully inflated bed and she was not a child in Corcoran anymore. Her 42-year-old son was making her breakfast on Mother's Day.

AUTHOR'S NOTE

When an author publishes a collection of stories, people invariably ask "What are they about?" It is an impossible question to answer, really, because the "they" in question is a mélange of diverse ideas and moods conceived by the author over months or years. In the case of the nine stories in this volume, I *could* say that they are simple fantasy and realistic stories without hidden messages, meant only to entertain the reader but that would spoil the fun of looking for hidden meanings, anagrams and possibly a character based on yourself. Talking animals, and in one case, a talking plant, is a favorite subject for me and there are four such stories in this volume; just the places to expect allegorical meanings to be craftily hidden.

The lead story, *Burnt Corn*, is a fantasy piece intended as an amusing tale exploring the question "Can an intra-genus affair between a hare and a rabbit bring love and happiness?" The longest story in the collection, *Three Suns on the Horizon*, is a mostly true adventure tale, a Londonesque account of two old geologists trying to survive above of the Arctic Circle. *I, Agave* derives from the author's reflections related to a trip to the village of Tequila in Jalisco, Mexico and *Bird of Constant Sorrow* deals with speculations about a lonely male cardinal in the author's Texas backyard. Two entries in the volume, *Good Morning Lisbon* and *The Corcoran Dream* are nostalgic tales recalling people and places that entered the author's life in Portugal and a distant summer of vanished youth spent in the cotton fields of the southern San Joaquin Valley of California.

Ha'boon is a futuristic piece that examines a time in which baboon organs can be transplanted to humans without fear of infection, rejection or simian side-effects. The remaining two stories, *Grotto of the Golden Snake* and *Canto do Virapuru* are dark tales, almost entirely fiction, set in Japan and equatorial Brazil. The latter, a mix of nostalgia, magic, an realism deriving from the writer's two years in Belém, Brazil.

So, there you have it from the author's mouth, nine recently written tales which I hope readers will enjoy. If you insist on theme, I would have to call it *diversity*, or better yet, *mélange*.

Remember, they are all fiction, but there is no harm in asking if any of the characters are based on you. However, you will find that most of the actors in these stories are not that attractive.

ABOUT THE AUTHOR

Dr. Lowell was born and raised on a small dairy farm outside of Modesto, California. He attended high school in Glendora, California and San Jose State University where he received a B.S. degree in Geology. His passion for minerals led him to the New Mexico Institute of Mining and Technology where he received a PhD degree in Geology three years later.

A long academic career followed at Southeast Missouri State, a two- year posting at a Brazilian university, and eight years at University of Texas-Arlington. During this period, Dr. Lowell published 104 scientific works, consulted for mineral industry, presented research at conferences all over the world and lived in both Brazil and Portugal.

Since retirement, Dr. Lowell has occupied himself writing short fiction and has six stand-alone works in publication (Full Moon Publishing). His stories are often set in Alaska, Portugal or Brazil and involve odd characters, geology and, sometimes, talking animals! He reads widely and is especially fond of 19th century classics; his favorite novels include *Don Quixote, Les Miserables, and My Ántonia*. Dr. Lowell and his wife Vicki live in Arlington, Texas; their adult children live nearby.

www.ingramcontent.com/pod-product-compliance
Lightning Source LLC
Chambersburg PA
CBHW050750250626
47155CB00005B/1995